ChangelingPress.com

Raven's Song (Arcane Talents)
An Arcane Talents Prequel
Angela Knight

Raven's Song (Arcane Talents)
An Arcane Talents Prequel
Angela Knight

ISBN: 978-1-60521-890-8

Publisher:
Changeling Press LLC
315 N. Centre St.
Martinsburg, WV 25404
ChangelingPress.com

Printed in the U.S.A.

Editor: Jean Cooper
Cover Artist: Angela Knight

The individual stories in this anthology have been previously released in E-Book format.

Table of Contents

Raven's Song (Arcane Talents)
An Arcane Talents Prequel
Angela Knight

Raven Garland is a rock star with a voice that is literally magical. She's also got a serious problem: she's being stalked by her ex. Ewan Bradley's magical abilities and powerful father make him a deadly threat, forcing her to hire a seductive bodyguard with powers of his own. Nate Carter can use his Primo magic to increase his physical strength to superhuman levels -- and he needs every bit of that power to keep Raven alive. Besides her nasty ex, there's the lethal costar with anger issues and a mystical link to a bulletproof tiger.

To make matters worse, Nate is slowly falling in love with his client. The passion seems mutual, but Raven's love affairs have a notoriously short shelf life. For all his strength, Nate doesn't think he can take becoming her latest fling. Raven wants her handsome bodyguard as far more than a temporary lover, but how can she convince him to trust her when he knows her magical voice can make him believe whatever she wants. Nate knows in real life, the good guy doesn't always get the girl.

My Feral Heart

Deep in my Feral heart
Where all my passions start,
I feel your magic's call.
I want to give you all,
All my Feral heart.

You make my hunger roar
All I want is more.
See the gold of my eyes?
I tell you no lies --
I'm the cat you're looking for.

I taste your Arcane kiss,
and feel your fire hiss
As your magic heats my skin,
You make me want to sin
Deep in my Feral Heart.

You make my hunger roar
All I want is more.
See the gold of my eyes?
I tell you no lies --
I'm the cat you're looking for.

See me stalk you in the dark
Listen to my passion growl
'Cause I wanna hear you yowl.
Feel your power spark
Deep in your Feral Heart.

You make my hunger roar
All I want is more.
See the gold of my eyes?
I tell you no lies --
I'm the cat you're looking for.

Chapter One

Nathan Carter watched the woman he loved kiss another man.

Raven Garland lay sprawled among sheets of crimson silk, eyes closed, full lips parted on a gasp as the muscular blond braced above her. Her lover pressed biting kisses to the angle of her delicate jaw, and she gripped his bare shoulders, scarlet nails digging into his skin. Her sweat-sheened body seemed to glow in the light from dozens of candles that surrounded the brass bed, clustered on the floor, or arranged on the nightstand among drifts of white rose petals.

All the while, her voice -- that amazing three-octave, Grammy-winning voice -- poured from hidden speakers in a sensual purr. "Deep in my Feral heart, where all my passions start, I feel your magic's call..."

Nate could certainly feel her magic call as he stood in the shadows of the huge room. A call he desperately wanted to answer, even as his common sense told him to stay the fuck away.

Unfortunately, his instincts also told him her lover was going to be a problem. A big, powerfully muscled bastard, Gary Handle was the kind of guy women like Raven would be drawn to.

He wore his dishwater blond hair cropped in a military brush cut that accentuated his square jaw and hawkish nose. He had the gold irises that marked him as a Feral, though his eyes were a bit too small to balance that wide mouth. Good-looking enough, but there was something about Gary that made Nate's combat-honed instincts howl.

Raven didn't seem to sense the danger as she stared up at him, entranced, her lush body relaxed and yearning in his arms.

Nate wanted to touch her like that. Wanted to feel the weight of those full breasts, her long dancer's legs gripping his hips. Just like that.

He also wanted to haul Gary the hell off her and drive his fist into the bastard's nose. The crunch of cartilage would be intensely satisfying.

Breathing in hard, Nate fought the absurd jealousy. *She's a client. What kind of idiot bodyguard gets jealous of a client? She doesn't see me as anything but hired muscle. And she's right.*

His inner Neanderthal didn't give a shit. Nate closed his eyes, trying to control the waves of irrational emotion...

And stiffened. In the darkness behind his closed eyelids, Raven glowed like a torch, the aura of her Bard magic bright to Nate's Talent senses.

But above her, where Gary Handle should be, a glowing tiger crouched, ears laid back, tail lashing as it stared down at her with vicious intensity.

The spirit of Gary's dead cat wanted to take a bite out of Raven. *Fuck, fuck, fuck!*

"Cut!" Roger Timmons called from his place beside the studio camera, his voice taut with frustration. Around him, the rest of the video crew -- the two camera operators, the sound engineer, the lighting crew -- even the hair and makeup girl -- looked just as impatient. "Gary, you flashed her suit top again. We're trying to create the illusion Raven's naked, and we can't do that if fabric shows." He glowered, eyes narrowing as he bit off every word. "Keep one hand over the top, damn it."

Handle gave Raven a glittering glare in the

blazing lights of the soundstage. "Why don't you just take it off? Then we wouldn't have to worry about showing it."

"No, just my nipples," Raven said, irritation edging her tone. Even so, her voice sounded rich and seductive, silken as the sheets. And she wasn't even drawing on the Bard magic that had made her one of the hottest rock stars of the decade.

Gary opened his mouth on a snarl that sounded as if he were on the edge of manifesting his tiger. "You..."

Nate tensed, his bodyguard instincts howling. *Too far away. I'm too damn far away if he goes for her...* He jolted forward a step.

"Fuck it, take ten," Timmons said in disgust. "I don't like this angle anyway. Jack, maybe we should try positioning the camera a little lower..." He turned to the cinematographer, a grizzled older man who was staring at Gary with a troubled frown. Apparently, Jack didn't like the looks of the Feral either.

"Whatever, man." Gary rolled from the bed. Giving Raven a glare, he stalked off the bedroom set platform, wearing only a Speedo and a layer of baby oil.

"Jerk," Raven muttered, and sat up, the sheet falling to her lap, revealing her strapless red bikini. She hunched forward, raking her hands through her hair, her expression tight. The position showed too much gorgeous cleavage for Nate's peace of mind, and he dragged his gaze away.

He'd done that a lot over the year he'd been Raven's bodyguard. She fascinated him with that disciplined dancer's body, quick mind, and the Bard magic that pulsed around her when she performed.

None of which made it easy to stay focused on

his job: protecting her from Ewan Bradley, the psycho ex who'd been terrorizing her.

Now, watching Gary pace like a literal tiger in a cage, Nate had the nasty feeling her stalker might be a lot less dangerous than her costar.

Nate had done a background check on Handle when Raven decided to hire him. On paper he'd looked fine. As a Feral, Gary's Talent let him form psychic links with animals. And he was even better at it than most. One test had pegged him in the top two percent in the country, which was why the U.S. Arcane Corps had been so eager to recruit him. He'd done well enough in training to be issued one of the Corps' rare tiger Familiars. The cat was bred to be every bit as magically powerful as he was, and the two had been able to achieve a successful psychic link. Working together, Handle and his Familiar could create a manifestation -- a tiger shell formed of pure magic he could wear like a suit of armor. It gave him the strength, claws and fangs of the real beast, as well as making him bulletproof.

Handle was only an inch or so shorter than Nate's six-four, so he outweighed Raven by at least seventy-five pounds. Add the tiger to that... *This situation could get really ugly, really fast.*

One-on-one, Nate figured he could take Handle. Trouble was, you were never one-on-one with a Feral, because the guy's cat could manifest before you threw a punch. Nate was good, but not good enough to go toe-to-toe with a bulletproof tiger.

"Hey, Roger..." Raven rose and grabbed the silk robe that had been hidden under the pillows, shrugging it on over her bikini. "I've got an idea..."

The director looked around as she headed for him. "Of course you do." He sounded frustrated. For once, Nate didn't blame him.

"Who wants to make a bet on when Roger loses his shit?" Kara Mayfield asked, dry amusement in her voice. She and Monique Elliot had joined Nate in an out-of-the-way corner of the soundstage to watch the shooting.

Like Raven, Kara wasn't particularly tall, though her lush figure made the most of her ripped designer jeans and snug yellow tee. She wore her short hair sculpted into gleaming waves that made her huge, dark eyes look even bigger in her pretty oval face. "Personally, I give it half an hour before ol' Rog goes off like Mount St. Helens. Gary's turned this shoot into an epic cluster."

"Like a monkey fucking a football," Monique agreed. The backup singer had a voice like aged whiskey, smoky and hypnotic with Bard talent. A tall, statuesque forty-year-old with rich, dark brown skin, she wore low-rise jeans and a crop top that revealed the gold glint of a belly-button ring. "You know, I could understand having trouble with the choreography. Dancing isn't Gary's Talent." They'd ended up canning the whole routine because the Feral couldn't remember the steps. "But how hard could it be for a straight boy to pretend to make love to Raven fuckin' Garland?"

"And the more he screws up," Nate said grimly, "the madder he gets."

"He's not nearly as mad as Roger." Kara shook her head. "They blew half the shoot budget on footage they can't even use. Raven told me she regrets casting him."

Monique slanted Nate a sly grin. "Maybe they should have cast you."

Knowing when he was being teased, Nate

drawled, "I'm a Primo, not a cat cowboy." Just as Bards sang to focus their magic, Primos used movement -- usually dance, though martial arts worked too.

"At least you'd have been able to learn the damn choreography."

"Not a dancer either." No son of Sarah Carter's would ever dance professionally, Primo or not. Not if he ever wanted to come to Christmas dinner again.

"Which makes zero sense. How can you be a Primo and not dance? Especially with all..." Kara swept a gesture up and down his body. "*That.*"

"Damn waste, is what it is." Monique's dark eyes twinkled at him. "One thing's for sure -- you wouldn't have had any trouble with this scene."

"And neither would Raven." Kara grinned, white teeth flashing. "Probably wouldn't even care about the nipples."

Nate cleared his throat. "Yeah, right. Seriously..."

"Honey, we're completely serious. You are way hotter than Pussy Pal," Monique said, and both women cracked up.

Nate eyed them, suspecting he was turning red. "If you could take a break from giving me hell, would you do me a favor? Close your eyes and check Gary's aura." He pointed across the soundstage at the Feral, who was still pacing restlessly.

Kara was an Arcanist, a magical heavyweight who could channel magic through sigils, drawings or spell circles. She might spot something he couldn't see.

Kara lost the grin in a hurry. "You think we've got a problem?"

"Maybe."

Both women frowned and closed their eyes. Monique's arched brows rose. "Well, shit."

"I don't know jack about Familiars, but if that cat was flesh and blood, I'd be running the fuck away," Kara agreed, "And I really do not like the way it's looking at Raven."

"Neither do I." Nate blew out a breath. "I think it's reacting to Gary's frustration, and its anger is intensifying his. And his cranks the cat's." He drew a circle in the air, illustrating the feedback loop. "Round and round it goes, where it stops... We could be fucked."

"You need to warn Raven and Timmons." Monique pursed her full lips. "Who will not be happy."

"Nope. But Timmons needs to be a lot more careful before he sets that tiger off."

Kara snorted. "Especially since Roger's dial is pretty much stuck on *asshole*."

As Nate started toward the corner of the soundstage where Raven and the director were talking, Kara called, "Good luck. You're gonna need it."

"Gee, thanks." He'd need more than luck if Gary lost it. The last time he'd gone up against a Feral, he'd damn near died. And he'd been much better armed then.

The glowing tiger leaped at him, blazing like a jet's afterburners, its roar revealing fangs the length of his fingers. Clawed forepaws blurred toward his face...

The Ruger P90 in his shoulder holster suddenly felt like a water pistol.

"... And that's when Gary could manifest the tiger," Raven was saying as he approached.

The director nodded judiciously. "It would make for good visuals."

Or more bloodshed than I even want to think about. "May I have a word?"

Timmons turned and stared up at him in offended surprise. He was a small man, thin and balding, with a prominent nose and a bushy George Lucas-style beard. The Lucas thing was probably deliberate. "You do realize we're in the middle of a shoot?"

"Do you realize you're about to step on a land mine?" Nate asked bluntly. He was usually more diplomatic with clients, but you couldn't sugarcoat a problem this bad. And Timmons was a hardheaded bastard to begin with. "If you'd give me a moment of your time, maybe we can all avoid the blast."

The director's eyes widened. "Is this about that asshole Ewan?" His gaze flicked around in worry. "Is he here?"

"No, I'm talking about Gary."

"Gary?" Timmons's brows lowered. "Oh, give me a break. Yeah, he's a prick, but..."

"He's more than a prick. He's dangerous."

"Bullshit. I..."

"If Nate says there's a problem," Raven interrupted, watching Nate with a frown, "there's a problem."

"Bull. Shit," the director repeated.

She shot Timmons a cool look, and he visibly remembered he was dealing with one of the biggest rock stars in the industry. He cursed. "Fine. Why's he so damn dangerous?"

Before Nate could answer, the director turned to Andy Short, who was moving closer, his shoulder-mounted video camera trained on them. "What the fuck are you doing? This is *not* going in that MTV 'making of' thing. Go shoot Handle doing push-ups or hunting mice or whatever the fuck he's doing."

"Okay." The cameraman shrugged and

wandered off.

Timmons turned back to Nate. "So let's go. Why's the kitty dangerous?" He snapped his fingers in several impatient clicks. "Speed it up, Secret Service. Clock's ticking."

"I called one of my Arcane Corps buddies last night. Rich Miller's a Feral too, and he served with Handle. He said it's only been about six months since Gary's cat died in a helicopter crash during a training exercise. The Arcane Corps ended up giving him a medical discharge..."

"Yeah, and now he's got a furry roommate in his skull," Roger said impatiently. "Why the fuck do you think we hired him? First, 'My Feral Heart' is -- surprise! -- about a Feral. Second, we're gonna use his cat manifestation for the special effects. What's your point?"

"Rich told me that for the first year, a new Meld like Gary isn't in control of his cat. It's like a cross between puberty and 'roid rage -- with claws."

Raven frowned, looking uneasy. "Which would explain why Gary's still so pissed about yesterday."

"So much so that he's having trouble with today's shoot." He met the growing anger in Timmons's gaze. "If you keep riding him, you could ride him right over the edge. And since the Corps calls those guys 'tooth tanks' for a reason, none of us may survive the drop."

"Are you telling me how to manage my actors?"

"Yeah, because I know what you're dealing with -- and you don't have a clue. Look, I fought a Feral during Desert Storm. He was in Saddam Hussein's Republican Guard, and he killed three members of my patrol. I managed to save the other four with an M-16 and a fuck ton of luck. Let me repeat: Tooth. Tank. If

Gary loses his shit, my Ruger might as well be a straw and spitballs."

Raven looked uneasy. "What do you suggest we do?"

"Rich told me it'll be at least another year before Gary'll be safe to work with. That's why they discharged him to begin with -- he's dangerous. You need to hire another Feral."

"And throw out all the video I've already shot? Blow both my shooting schedule *and* my budget?" Timmons scoffed. "I don't fucking think so."

"Listen to me," Nate said, leaning in to force the smaller man to meet his eyes. "You're turning a tiger loose and trusting it not to eat your crew. This is going to end in lawsuits and blood. Hire someone else."

"There isn't anybody else," Roger shot back, his voice rising. "All the other available Ferals are either pug ugly or date from Vietnam. They're too Goddamn old to be Raven's love interest. This guy is perfect, and I'm not firing him."

"Is that worth risking everyone's life?" Nate snapped, out of patience. "Including Raven's and your own?"

"Gary's a decorated combat vet," Raven said in a voice so soothing, he felt his anger diminish. "I'm sure he doesn't want to hurt anyone. And if he has a problem, I can help him."

She's using her Talent to calm us both down, Nate realized. Sure enough, the fury was draining from the director's gaze too. *I just wish she'd use it to make Timmons listen.*

Earnest green eyes gazed into his. "I realize it's your job to keep me safe. But Gary needs both the work and a little understanding. If he loses control, I can calm him down."

"You have no idea how fast a Feral is. I do. You won't have time..."

Roger interrupted with a sneer, "You're *scared* of him. And here I thought you were supposed to be Billy Badass."

Raven slanted him a look. "Roger, you're not helping." She laid a hand on the center of Nate's chest. Her palm felt warm, there over his heart. Right. "Look, if there's a problem, I'll sing."

He eyed her, his temper beginning to steam, magic or no magic. "You're spending the whole scene in his arms. If he goes for you, you won't get a note out of your mouth. I saw a Feral just like him maul three armed Marines to death..."

"I. Am. Not. Firing. Him," Roger cut in. "*You*, on the other hand..."

"Nate doesn't work for you," Raven told him, her voice icy. "He works for me, and he's not going anywhere."

"And *I'm* not firing Gary."

"Fine!" Nate ground his teeth. Short of picking Raven up and carrying her out, all he could do now was try to minimize the body count. And pray. "Raven, if Gary goes off, don't try to run. That'll trigger his cat, and he'll chase you. Don't look him in the eye if you have to sing. His cat will interpret that as aggression. I'll distract him so you get out." *I'll probably die doing it, but that fucker isn't getting you.*

"And they say Bards are drama queens." Timmons scoffed. "Don't listen to this idiot. He's just trying to prove you need him. Look, go back in and talk to Gary. Do your Bard thing and calm him down. And get your makeup touched up. It's smeared."

Raven hesitated, frowning up at Nate, then shook her head and walked off.

As soon as she was out of earshot, Roger rounded on him. "I realize you want in her pants. I don't blame you. But do it on your own Goddamn time!"

Nate ground his teeth. "*I'm not trying to get in her pants.* I'm trying to keep her breathing. And *you* with her."

Roger glared. "I'm about this far from calling the studio and raising hell until they make her fire you, no matter what she says. Your job is to protect her, not interfere with my shoot."

"Have it your way," Nate growled, throwing his hands up. "But I'm telling you, if I'm right and Gary snaps, don't panic and don't run. I'll buy you time to get away."

Roger laughed in his face. "You really are scared shitless of him! You've got everybody convinced you're some big war hero, but you're just a fucking coward."

Goaded, Nate snapped, "I've got a Bronze Star that says otherwise. Which I got killing that fucking Feral to save my team. And if you call me a coward one more time…"

The little man took a step back. "When this shoot is over, I'm going to do everything in my power to get rid of your arrogant ass."

"And until then, I'm going to do everything in mine to keep your arrogant ass alive."

"Yeah, well, you'd better quit interfering with this damn shoot or I'll call security and have you thrown the fuck out!" The director whirled and marched away, narrow shoulders squared.

Moron. Roger reminded him of an idiot Second Lieutenant he'd had during the war. The little prick had been insecure as fuck and desperate to prove his authority. As the dickhead's sergeant, Nate had spent Desert Storm trying to both keep the bastard alive and prevent him from killing his own men to prove the size of his flyspeck balls. *Aaaand... I've left Raven alone a little too long with the furry psycho.* He broke into a long, ground-eating stride, passing the director. And wished for his M16.

* * *

Raven stood with her eyes closed, frowning as she watched the tiger pace circles around Handle. Nate was right. The cat did look agitated.

Something glowing appeared in her peripheral vision, bright and beautiful. The pattern of the aura -- the magic strongest around the legs and arms -- told her it was a Primo, though none of her dancers was on the set today.

Nate.

His magic didn't glow as brightly as Gary's -- Ferals were the most powerful of the Talents -- but he still had more juice than any dancer she'd ever met.

Yet he swore he didn't dance. What was up with that? She could have no more given up magic than she could give up breathing.

She opened her eyes, and the sheer impact that handsome face hit her all over again. Nate's short sable hair looked disordered, as if he'd been raking his hands through it in frustration and worry. His eyes were a clear, cool gray in a face that appeared carved from granite, all chiseled angles and cleft chin, his nose a long, aggressive jut. His mouth looked full, sensual, especially framed by five-o'clock shadow. It made her want to kiss him. Explore the contrast between the prickle of stubble and the silk of his lips.

He wore jeans and a black tee, along with the lightweight black jacket he wore to conceal his shoulder holster. The combo made his shoulders look a mile wide. Which wasn't far from the truth. He often worked out with her, and the sight of a sweat-slicked Nate in nothing but pair of damp nylon shorts...

I will not hit on my bodyguard. I will not hit on my bodyguard. She needed to write that on a blackboard somewhere. About a thousand times.

Raven had known a lot of handsome men, kissed them, dated them, made love to them. Hell, look at Ewan. Her ex-husband was even more gorgeous than Nate, at least on the outside. Nate was all rough edges and zero talent for diplomacy. Yet for all that, for all his strength and lethal competence, he lacked the sense of ticking danger that had so fascinated her about Ewan when she'd been young and stupid. Before she'd learned what "bad boy" really meant.

Nate was *good* all the way to his bedrock-steady soul.

For a moment his gaze met hers across the soundstage. Need rolled over her, as it so often did in his presence. *Falling for your bodyguard is such a cliché*, Raven thought, impatient with herself. *It didn't even work for Whitney Houston.* Nate was the exact same kind of noble idiot as Whitney's movie hero. *And here I am, being just as dumb.* She started toward him anyway.

"All right, folks!" Roger said, dropping into his director's chair. "Let's get this thing in the can. Places."

Nate turned away to head back to his favorite corner... and froze, his shoulders stiffening.

Gary was staring at him from a foot away. "If you don't quit eye-fucking me, boy," he said, Alabama thick in his voice, "I'm gonna fuck you right back."

She expected Nate to say something quiet and menacing, which was how he usually handled dickheads. Instead he turned his head, looking away from the Feral, though his shoulders were square, his body relaxed and ready. Trying to avoid triggering the man's cat.

Closing her eyes, Raven saw magic gathering around Nate's right hand, the glow building until his skin seemed to smoke. He was calling power. Why? *If he doesn't use his magic to dance, what* does *he use it for?*

Eyes still closed, she looked beyond the blaze of his aura. The tiger crouched, snarling. It was huge, its head level with Nate's rib cage. *If it jumps him…*

"Yeah, I figured you'd back down, you chickenshit," Gary sneered. "What are *you* looking at?"

Raven realized he was talking to her and snapped her eyes open. Temper stung her at the contempt in her costar's golden eyes. She gave serious thought to firing him on the spot -- fuck Roger's precious budget. After Ewan, she didn't play doormat to any man.

Until she remembered Nate's warning. *If you keep riding him, you could ride him right over the edge.* She breathed in, calling power, and poured soothing peace into her voice. "Your cat doesn't look happy."

To her shock, her magic seemed to splash right off Gary's sneer. "No, because your asshole boyfriend pisses him off. But don't worry, I can control him. Come on, let's finish this." He turned and started back toward the bed.

Raven followed, but as she passed Nate, she looked up at him. His hard gaze was fastened on the back of Gary's head, flat and cold. And very, very grim.

A chill rolled over her. *Nate doesn't think he can take Gary.* She'd never seen any situation her bodyguard hadn't been able to handle -- and that included Ewan at his menacing worst. Even cops had been a little intimidated when her ex-husband went into his psycho act. Nate had merely looked bored.

But Gary Handle worried him.

So I'll just have to be ready to sing if Gary blows. It wouldn't be the first time she'd had to use magic to control a violent asshole. There'd been days Raven's Bard magic had been the only reason Ewan hadn't killed her. *I can handle Gary.*

Hell, she'd once enchanted an entire Super Bowl stadium crowd just by singing "The Star-Spangled Banner." Thousands had stood there with tears rolling down their faces, lost in her magic. *Yeah, I can control Gary.*

I hope.

Her own voice began rolling from the speakers again so they could sync their motions to it. "Deep in my Feral heart Where all my passions start, I feel your magic's call..."

Reluctantly, she slid into bed with the big Feral, uncomfortably aware of his size, his strength -- and the way he was looking at her. *Like he's thinking of taking a bite. And not in the fun way.*

"*You're going to want to run,*" Nate's voice said in her memory. "*Don't.*"

She already wanted to run. But after Ewan, she'd sworn her running days were over, so she gave Gary a defiant smile.

"Stand by," Roger called. "Roll tape."

"Rolling," The cameraman replied. The two studio cameras' indicator lights came on -- they were shooting simultaneously from different angles for this shot.

A production assistant moved in front of the two cameras and clapped a slate.

"Annnnd... Action."

Gary yanked her into his arms, his eyes wide and glittering as he took her mouth in a kiss so hard, it ground her lips painfully against her teeth. She jerked with a muffled sound of protest. *This isn't how the scene's supposed to start!*

A low rumble vibrated the air: a growl. The tiger spirit.

Raven closed her eyes to find the cat staring at her, its huge head looming over her like a harvest moon. She couldn't tell if it wanted to fuck her or eat her -- and she didn't like either option. Tasting blood, she realized Gary had bitten her lip. She planted her fists against his chest and tried to shove him away. "Get off!"

"Cut!" Roger said, annoyed. "Raven, this is supposed to be a love scene. Gary, could you dial back on the Charles Manson?"

She opened her eyes to see Gary giving the director a murderous glare.

Roger didn't appear to notice. "Once more, from the top. Roll tape."

What felt like a wasp stung her shoulder, and she jerked as a drop of liquid rolled down her arm. Looking down, Raven saw the tips of Gary's fingers glowed gold. A chill rolled over her from heels to hairline. He'd manifested three-inch claws, and they were digging into her skin. She was bleeding. "You cut me!" She tried to jerk free of his hold, but he didn't release her. "Let go!"

"You think you can control *me*?" Gary snarled. "Think you can sing your little song and I'll just roll over for you?"

Shit, he heard us.

"Cut!" Roger roared. Tearing off his headset, he stalked toward them. "What's the problem?"

Raven stared up at Gary's furious face. "He manifested claws," she said, fear making her voice faint.

"I did not!" Smirking, Gary spread his hands, displaying clawless fingers.

"Then why am I bleeding, asshole?" From the corner of her eye, she saw Nate start forward, his expression grim, his right hand sliding under the lapel of his leather jacket. Ready to draw the gun in his shoulder holster.

Roger frowned at the shallow punctures. "At least they're not deep." He turned an icy gaze on Gary. "If you have any desire for that film career you talked about when I hired you, you'd better not try that bullshit again. Or you are fucking *gone*." He started to turn as if to head back to his chair.

"I thought you were worried about your budget. I thought I was the only Feral who wasn't too old to fuck her." Gary rolled out of bed to tower over the smaller man, lips twisted in a snarl.

Yeah, he'd heard them. Roger realized it too, judging by the way he froze and went pale.

Well, Nate warned us, Raven thought numbly. *Hope we'll all live to hear the "I told you so."*

Gold light exploded around the Feral as his tiger manifested. Roger leaped back with a startled yell. Roaring, Gary pounced on him like a cat on a hamster, slamming into the director and riding him to the cement floor.

Roger threw up both arms to protect his head. "No! Get off..."

The tiger tore into him.

Chapter Two

Massive glowing jaws clamped onto Roger's arm with the crunch of splintering bone. The director howled in terrified agony as Gary whipped the cat's huge glowing head back and forth. Trying to rip his arm off.

Sing! I've got to sing! Raven clawed for her magic, but all that emerged was a choked croak. *Oh, shit shit shit!*

Roger's howls mixed with the crew's panicked screams as they ran for the exits, getting in Nate's way as he fought to get to Roger. Raven might have run too, but she knew Nate would stay. Nate would fight. *I've got to sing!*

"911!" Nate bellowed over Roger's screams, dodging a fleeing cameraman, then leaping over a production assistant who was trying to crawl away. "Somebody call 911!"

"Raven!" Monique and Kara grabbed her arms and hauled her out of the bed. She hadn't even seen them approach. "Let's get out of here!"

"*No!*" Raven jerked free of her friends' hands. Nate wouldn't leave. He'd try to save Roger even if he died doing it. "*I've got to sing!*" She drew breath as her magic finally, finally responded...

As if sensing the rise of her power, the tiger released the director's mangled arm and wheeled toward her. The cat roared and charged her, leaving Roger writhing, clutching his mangled arm.

All three women shrieked. Raven squeezed her eyes closed, groping frantically for the power that terror had stripped away. Behind her closed lids, she saw the tiger crouch, Gary coiled inside its glowing shell, a vicious grin twisting his face.

We're dead.

Nate plunged out of nowhere, his right hand a ball of white-hot fire around the shadow of his gun. He slammed into the tiger shell's back, staggering the man inside it even as his fireball fist swung, punching into the cat's glowing head in an explosion of mystical sparks. Gary roared, the sound half-man, half-cat...

Nate fired, the gun's bark a thin, flat crack in the studio's open space.

The tiger winked out, cut off in mid-roar. Simply vanished as Nate slammed through the space it had occupied, smashing into Gary. Her bodyguard hit the floor in a controlled roll, but the Feral went down like a bag of wet cement.

Gary came to rest with his face turned toward her. His forehead was a red ruin from the bullet's exit. Raven stared at it, unable to look away, feeling as if she hovered somewhere outside her body.

Nate flipped to his feet like an Olympic gymnast. Raven couldn't seem to look away from Gary's shattered skull, the fragments of bone and brain surrounding his head as he lay in a boneless sprawl.

"Holy Jesus," Kara murmured, sounding as shell-shocked as Raven felt.

Minutes before, Gary had held her, kissed her. *And tried to rake me open with his claws because I pissed him off. And now he's dead. But if we'd listened to Nate and fired him, he might be alive.* She felt sick.

"Oh, God oh God oh God!" the director screamed, writhing in a pool of his own blood. She dimly realized he'd been screaming all along. She just hadn't heard him. "Help me! Christ, fuck, it hurts, it hurts!" His unbitten hand pawed uselessly at his savaged right arm as it pumped blood onto the floor. *Shit, he's bleeding out!*

"I've got you, Roger," Nate shouted over his screams as he hurried over, unbuckling his belt as he dropped to his knees beside the injured man. He looked at Raven and her shell-shocked, staring friends. "Hey!" The ringing snap of his voice jolted her out of her fog. He whipped off his belt, and for a moment she had no idea why. "I need some help here, ladies! We've got to get this bleeding stopped or he'll die before the ambulance gets here. He needs a tourniquet. Find me an ink pen."

Raven stared, not seeing the connection. Feeling stupid and slow. "A pen? What..."

"For the tourniquet," Kara told her. "Look around." Her friend began scanning the room. Prodded, Raven started scanning the floor, the shelves and worktables that stood around the soundstage...

Kneeling, Nate cinched the belt around the director's mangled arm. "This is going to hurt, Roger, but it will keep you alive." He looked up. "Find that fucking pen! A screwdriver, *anything* that's straight and hard. I don't care."

Raven spotted a clipboard lying abandoned and started toward it, almost colliding with Andy Short. She hadn't even realized he hadn't left with the others. He had his shoulder mounted camera trained on Nate and Roger.

"Fuck," the documentarian whispered, as if to himself. His eyes were wide and avid. "This is some great shit. Gonna be worth a fortune."

"What is *wrong* with you?" Raven demanded, outraged.

He looked away from the camera's viewfinder to curl his lip at her. "Some of us ain't millionaire rock stars."

Spotting a pen in his shirt pocket, she snatched it.

"Give me that pen, you vulture." She whirled and hurried to hand it to Nate, who stuck it through the belt he'd cinched around Roger's bloody arm and began to twist.

The director howled in agony. "What the fuck are you doing? Stop! Jesus!"

"This is a tourniquet. Otherwise you're going to bleed to death. He severed something major." The two were surrounded by a spreading puddle of crimson. And Roger's arm... Oh, God, it looked like raw meat, bone showing through the torn...

Without looking away from what he was doing, Nate ordered, "Raven, find a phone and call an ambulance."

"Yeah. Yeah, I'll just..." Blindly, she turned for the door. Jesus, she'd never seen so much blood...

The door swung open just as she reached for it. Jack, the head cameraman, stuck his head in and hissed a curse. "I called 911. Ambulance and cops are on the way."

"Good." His expression tight and grim, Nate gave the tourniquet another ruthless twist.

"Motherfucker!" Roger writhed, teeth clenched around a scream.

"Hang on," Nate told him, "Help's coming. They'll load you up with such good drugs, you won't know what planet you're on."

"Stupid. So stupid. Should... should have listened... you." The director stared up at Nate, his gaze fevered, his paper-pale face wet with sweat. His shaking voice was so high, it didn't sound like him at all. "Saved my... my life. After what I said... you saved me. 'M so fuckin' stupid."

"Don't worry about it." Nate gave the director a tight smile. "They've called an ambulance. You'll be fine."

"Gonna lose this arm. Aren't I? Gonna lose it." Tears ran down his drawn, white face.

I have to do something, Raven thought. *I have to help. Sing. I can sing.* She reached for her power and called up a memory of walking on the beach, listening to the waves roll in, watching sunlight dance over the water. She gathered up all that peace of that memory and poured it all into her voice on a river of magic. "When you're weary, feeling small, When tears are in your eyes..."

She kept belting out "Bridge Over Troubled Water," until she felt it take hold, rolling through Roger's aura, slowing the agonized scarlet churn over his arm. He looked up at her, glazing eyes locked on her face, his lips parting as her magic began to insulate him from his own suffering. *Yeah, this I can do. It's something.* She gave the song everything she had -- all the magic, all the passion, all the memories of that perfect summer day when the sun was hot on her shoulders and the salt breeze blew cool on her face.

Pumping every bit of power she had into her voice, she sang as she'd never sung before. Not cutting a record, not for that Super Bowl crowd, not even for the Grammys.

She barely noticed as the rest of the crew filtered back in, drawn despite the blood, despite Gary's corpse. They sank into chairs or just sat right down on the blood-splattered floor, staring at her, rapt, their trauma forgotten.

She kept singing, trying to make up for her own failure and what it had cost Roger, herself, even Gary. Gary, who'd served his country and lost himself doing it. Gary, who'd kissed her. She couldn't let herself wonder if she could have saved him if she'd kept her

head. *Would Nate have had to kill him if I hadn't frozen?*
No. Not thinking that. All I've got to do is sing.

* * *

Nate staggered out into the hallway, feeling stoned as hell. Raven's voice poured through the open doorway in a cascade of peace and love until all he wanted to do was sit down on the floor and listen. But there were things he had to do, so he fought that drugging voice, digging deep into the discipline he'd learned when his father had made Nate and his brothers do Karate *katas* until every muscle ached.

"*You don't give up,*" his father had told them. Nate must have been about eight at the time. "*Carters never, never give up. When you give up, you fail the people who're counting on you. The people you love.*"

I made you proud today, Dad, he thought numbly, as he forced himself to close the door on Raven's seductive voice. The reduction in volume helped clear his head, though he still wanted to stand and listen. Damn, he'd known she was powerful, but this was Talent on a whole different level. He turned and staggered off down the hall, his thoughts growing sharper the farther he got. *I've got to call Mom and Dad and tell them what happened before they see it on the morning news.* Not the way to find out your son had just killed a man.

But first he had to talk to his partner.

Spotting a phone hanging on the wall, he headed over to pluck it off the hook. He felt so fuzzy from a combination of magical backlash and Raven's song that it took him two tries to dial his partner's number.

"Robertson residence!" a cheerful teenage voice said. Sherrie, Bruce's teenage daughter.

He could hear approaching sirens. *Running out of time.*

Nate leaned harder into the wall. His muscles were shaking, and his head was pounding from the aftermath of the punch. "Let me talk to your dad," he managed.

"Uncle Nate? Is that you? Oh, crap!" It sounded as if she'd turned away from the phone. "Daddy! Daddy, something's wrong with Uncle Nate!"

Well, she wasn't wrong.

A couple of moments later, Bruce's deep, familiar voice came on the line. "Nate, what's up?"

Nate hooked his hand around the base of the phone on its wall mount and used it to keep himself on his feet. "I just shot Gary Handle. He mauled the director and was going for Raven, so I shot him."

There was a long, appalled silence. "Are you hurt? You don't sound right."

Nate let the side of his head rest on the wall's cool plaster. "Had to use the fist. My Ruger wasn't going to get through his manifestation, so I punched it in."

"And it worked?" Bruce sounded astonished.

"Yeah, surprised me too." He sighed. "The cops and the ambulance are on the way -- I can hear sirens. Look, they're probably going to take me into custody while they investigate. Raven's going to need protection. I don't trust fucking Ewan Bradley not to go for her while I'm locked up."

Bruce's voice went matter-of-fact. "I'm on my way."

"Limo's parked behind the studio."

"I'll be there. Mary'll drive me." He paused. "You're going to need a lawyer."

"Raven's got a guy. She retained him after the shit started with Ewan."

An ambulance pulled to a screeching halt in front

of the door. "Gotta go. Ambulance is here." He hung up the phone and headed to the glass double door, toeing down the doorstop before making for the ambulance.

Two paramedics piled out. "What have we got?" one demanded as they ran to the back of the truck and swung open its doors.

"One victim. His arm was torn half off by a tiger manifestation."

The two men jerked around to stare at him, gaping. "Did you say *tiger?*" The medic's gaze flicked behind Nate as if looking for the cat.

"The Feral's dead. I had to shoot him -- he was about to kill my client. I put a tourniquet on the victim. He was bleeding out."

The stretcher hit the ground with a rattle as they pulled it to full height and began to wheel it toward the door. "Lead the way."

Nate obeyed, but when he pulled open the soundstage door, Raven's voice poured out. Both men broke step. Nate looked back and saw their eyes slide out of focus.

"That's Raven Garland..." one managed. "Jesus. Turn off... Turn off that recording..."

"It's not a recording. She's singing to the wounded man to help him control his pain."

"Oh, man, I'm getting high," the second EMT said, smiling, though his eyes looked vaguely worried. "Man. She's got to quit that."

"Yeah, she has that effect on me too," Nate said, and leaned in through the open door. "Raven, quit singing! The EMTs are here, and they can't concentrate with you doing that."

Silence fell, seeming to ring with silvery echoes of her voice.

"Wait... wait, what...?" Roger moaned. Then he screamed. "Oh, Jesus! Oh fuck, Christ! It hurts, it hurrrrrrts!"

The crew dashed inside. Before Nate could follow them, he heard more sirens. With a sigh, he pulled the Ruger from his shoulder holster and stepped out through the front doors again. He bent, putting the gun down on the sidewalk, then stepped well out of reach and knelt, lacing his hands behind his head.

And watched as what looked like half the LAPD leaped from their cars with their guns drawn.

* * *

Dazed from her own magic, Raven looked down at Roger and realized she knelt in a puddle of his blood. She'd sat down in it without noticing when she'd begun to sing. Now her butt felt sticky with drying gore, as did her legs, arms, and hands. Bloody handprints marked her skin. She felt her stomach heave.

"Get out of the way, people!" a beefy paramedic snapped as he and his partner wheeled a stretcher toward them. Raven tried to stand up, only to feel her knees give. She barely caught herself before she fell on her ass in the blood. She just sat there numbly, watching the paramedics work on Roger with the speed of people afraid their patient was dying. Within minutes, they lifted him onto the stretcher despite his hoarse howl of pain. He panted, head lolling, teeth clenched, eyes squeezed shut, as they wheeled him out.

Which was when the cops rushed in, guns drawn. "Everybody down on the floor!" one of them barked. "Stretch out, hands behind your heads. Now, people!"

Eyes widening, the crew threw intimidated looks

at the cops, then obeyed. Raven started to move back, but one of the cops said, "Get down *now!*"

Raven grimaced. "In the blood?" Her head was throbbing, the aftermath of all that magical effort taking its toll.

"No, not in the blood, that's evidence... Are you *naked?*"

"I'm wearing a bikini. It's just the same color as the blood."

"Why are you... Never mind. Just find a clear spot and stretch out."

She got up and moved clear of the blood, glancing around for Nate. He stood beside the open doors, having a very intense conversation with a cop who was busily taking notes. Nate too, was covered in blood, and judging by the look on the cop's face, he was a suspect.

Oh, hell no! Jolted out of her fugue, Raven started toward the pair.

A big hand grabbed her elbow. She looked around to see a short, balding uniformed cop with broad shoulders and a beer belly. "You heard the sergeant. On the floor."

"I need to talk to the officer with Nate. He's my bodyguard, and he saved my life. Gary's tiger was about to attack me -- he did attack Roger. Nate shot him. Otherwise we'd all be dead now."

The cop's hazel eyes widened. "What tiger? There's a tiger? It's loose?"

Raven grappled for patience. *What kind of idiot is this guy?* "Gary was a Feral with a tiger Familiar. I hired him for my music video, but he went off on the director, manifested his cat and tried to kill him. Nate shot him to protect the rest of us."

"Music video?" His brows lifted, and he smirked.

"Is that what you're calling it?"

Raven frowned at him, not understanding, until it hit her. *He thinks we were shooting porn.* Her tone frigid, she told him, "Yes, I'm Raven Garland."

The cop snorted. "Sure you..." He broke off as his eyes widened. "Shit. You are, aren't you? I didn't recognize you with blood all over your face. The dead guy was a Feral?"

Deciding she'd better start at the top, she started telling him the story as he took furious notes on a small pad. Just as she finished, a cop in a suit walked up, identified himself as Detective David Hudson, and asked her to start over. He too, scribbled notes and asked questions. Then he asked her to go through it again.

Halfway through the third repetition, she saw a second suited cop start handcuffing Nate. *Oh, hell no.* Raven headed toward them.

"Hold on," Hudson said, "I've got a few more..."

Ignoring him, she yelled at the other detective, "It was self-defense! Nate's my bodyguard, and Gary was about to attack me."

"And we'll turn him loose if we determine that's the case," Hudson told her. "But we've got to clear this up first."

But what if they didn't? How could she prove... Raven's eyes widened and she turned to the detective. "A guy's doing a video documentary on the shoot. Andy Short. The main cameras stopped rolling when Roger called cut, but maybe Andy was still shooting. His tape will prove I'm telling the truth."

Hudson stared at her. "Yeah, we want that tape. Where's this cameraman?"

Raven looked around, spotted Short, and hurried toward him. "Andy, did you shoot the attack on

Roger?"

The grizzled older man lifted a cool brow, not fazed in the least. "I was a combat photographer in Vietnam. Bet your ass I kept shooting."

Raven's shoulders sagged in relief.

"Why didn't you say you had video of the attack when I interviewed you?" The detective glared at the documentarian.

"Right offhand," Raven told him dryly, "I'd say he was planning to sell the tape to one of the networks."

The detective glowered at Andy. "Do the words 'obstruction of justice' mean anything to you, asshole? Show me that damn recording."

Realizing he was on thin ice, Andy carried his Betacam over to the studio TV monitor and hooked it up to the set's inputs, then began to rewind the tape, looking for the point when the attack began.

"Hey, Pate!" Hudson called, waving at his partner, who was about to march Nate out. "This guy says he shot video of the killing."

Pate headed over, still gripping Nate's upper arm. Her bodyguard looked tense with frustration and worry, the line of his broad shoulders tight.

They all watched silently as the video rolled. Raven felt herself go cold as Gary manifested and attacked Roger. Even Pate muttered a horrified curse as the tiger mauled the director before turning on Raven.

Nate raced into the frame, leaped impossibly high, and drove his gun into the manifestation. The gun went off with a thin crack, then the two went down, Nate rolling to his feet as the Feral collapsed.

"Back it up," Pate said. "Can you run it in slow motion?" He watched the video advance, then told

Short to pause it. "There!"

The frame showed Nate driving his gun into the tiger manifestation's glowing skull.

"How the fuck did you do that?" Pate demanded. "I saw Ferals fight in Vietnam. Those bastards are bulletproof. You should've bounced right off that cat and gotten eaten for your trouble."

Raven felt all the blood leave her face as she realized he was right. It hadn't hit her at the time -- she'd been too damn scared.

"Sheer desperation." Nate shrugged. "And I'm a Primo."

The cop's jaw dropped. "You're a *dancer*?"

"Primos can do more than dance. I'm a second-degree black belt in karate."

"Like Bruce Lee and shit?"

Nate's lips twitched. "Well, Bruce *was* a Primo."

"That still doesn't explain how you were able to do that." Hudson pointed at the screen.

"I knew a handgun bullet won't punch through a manifestation -- you need automatic rifle fire, and I didn't have that. So I concentrated my magic into my right hand so I could punch my weapon through his shell."

Pate frowned. "I didn't know you guys could do that. Aren't Primos supposed to be the weakest Talents? I do know Ferals are the strongest."

Nate shrugged. "Yeah."

"What the hell made you think it would work?"

"He was going to kill everybody in the room if it didn't. Since strong emotion can amplify magic, I figured it might work."

The detectives looked from Nate's face to hers, and something knowing flickered in their eyes. "Strong emotion," Pate said. "Yeah, I get that."

Nate eyed him right back. "I'm her bodyguard. It's my job."

"And you're definitely committed to your job." But there was respect in Hudson's gaze. "Pretty obvious this was self-defense."

They weren't going to charge him. The wave of relief was so intense, Raven's knees began to shake. She turned and staggered to the nearest chair. Collapsing into it, she braced her elbows on her knees and buried her face in her hands.

As if from a distance, she felt a big, warm hand cup the back of her neck. "You're okay," Nate said, his familiar voice deep and gentle. "It's going to be okay."

"Not for Roger," she said, tears stinging her eyes. "But at least they're not taking you to jail. I'd hug Andy if I didn't want to kick him in the ass."

"Why don't I get you a Coke? Your blood sugar has probably crashed from all that magic you threw around." He started to turn away.

A sudden wave of irrational panic made her grab his wrist. "Don't leave me!"

He studied her a moment. She must have looked pretty bad, because Nate looked around and waved across the soundstage. "Hey! Hey, Monique, would you get Raven a Coke out of the vending machine?"

"Sure," her friend called, and ducked out.

He sat down in the chair next to hers, his gaze steady. For once, he wasn't giving her that cool, professional-bodyguard stare. There was compassion in his eyes. And something warm and intense. Friendship or something more?

It looked like something more.

Raven leaned against his shoulder and curled her arms around his narrow waist. He felt so solid, so warm. She could have lost him if his gamble on his magic hadn't paid off. Gary would have ripped him apart.

He'd risked that for her. And she knew it wasn't just because he was her bodyguard.

* * *

Since the cops demanded his clothing as evidence, Nate grabbed the gym bag he kept in the back of the limo. He handed his clothes over to one of the cops, washed up in the men's shower and changed into his sweats. Feeling a bit better -- or at least no longer stinking of blood -- he decided it was time to call his parents.

He punched the number into one of the ubiquitous wall phones. His mother's familiar voice asked in alarm, "Nate? What's wrong?"

Nate winced, belatedly remembering it was three in the morning in Georgia. "I'm sorry to call this late, Mom. But there's been a problem."

"Are you all right?" She lifted her voice. "Steve, grab the other phone, it's Nate!"

A moment later, his dad picked up. "What's going on?

"Sorry to wake you. I just didn't want you to find out on the morning news."

"What happened?" There was no fear in the question, no alarm or anger. Just the cool tone Steve Carter used in every crisis. But then, he'd served in Vietnam.

His own tone clipped, Nate laid the sequence of events out for his father, all emotion divorced from the account as if he were giving a battlefield briefing.

"I *knew* it!" He could almost see his mother's thin hands wrapping in the phone cord in that nervous gesture she always used at times like this. "I told you that woman was going to get you killed. All those

Hollywood people are crazy! You should have become a cop."

"Yeah, but I didn't want have to shoot anybody again."

"And how did that work out for you?" she snapped.

"Sarah," his father said gently, "ease off."

"He needs to quit."

"And leave Raven to Ewan Bradley's tender mercies?" Nate snorted. "I don't think so."

"But..."

"We didn't raise our sons to turn their backs on women in trouble."

"That depends on whether they ask for it," his mother growled. "If Jennifer hadn't gotten hooked on Merlin, she wouldn't have gotten herself killed by that dealer of hers. That's what happens when you hang around Hollywood people trying to become a star." There was a sneer in her voice that was totally out of character.

The violent death of her beloved big sister was a wound his mother had never gotten over. Nate usually cut her some slack when it came to that particular psychic scar -- but his patience had worn thin. "Look, Raven's as anti-drug as you are. She certainly didn't ask to be terrorized by Ewan Bradley. This morning I opened a manila envelope that held a very ugly crime scene photo of a murdered woman. Raven's face had been pasted over the victim's. I am not going to abandon her. Especially not given that he damn nearly beat her to death when they were married. I don't care whether you like it or not."

"Nate, what if he hurts you?"

He snorted. "I hope he tries. I'd love giving him a taste of his own medicine. Look, Ma, I'm thirty-two years old. I no longer need parental guidance. Especially not when it comes to leaving..." *The woman I love.* "A client at the mercy of a sociopath. That's just not an option."

His father sighed. "I'd be disappointed if it were. Because that would mean we'd done something very wrong. And we didn't, did we, Sarah?"

"No," his mother said reluctantly. "We didn't."

* * *

Raven sat in an exhausted slump in her dressing room, finally clean and dressed, her wet hair disguised under a ball cap pulled low.

Kara bustled in, looking even grimmer than Raven felt. "Well, they've got the building surrounded," she announced. "I spotted live trucks from the ABC, CBS and NBC stations. There was even that asshole from the *Enquirer* and about a dozen paps." Like most stars, Raven had a love-hate relationship with the paparazzi. They could be useful when she needed to build buzz for an album, but they could also make her life a living hell whenever she didn't want the attention.

"Well, there's a shock -- not." Raven let her head fall back against the wall and closed her eyes. It felt like she'd used the last of her strength scrubbing the blood off. Even her hair had dried into gory clumps that had taken four shampoos to get clean.

Now her head throbbed in sullen pulses, an aftereffect of all the magic she'd used far too late to do anyone any real good. At least she'd given Roger a few pain-free minutes.

"I want to go to the hospital," she said to her closed eyelids.

Two glowing figures turned toward her -- Kara and Monique.

"Good idea. Open your eyes," Kara said as she obeyed, bending to study her face with a frown. "People have strokes after using that much magic. It was dumb. But at least your eyes are dilated the same. That's a good sign."

"No, I mean I want to visit Roger. This is just a little backlash. It's no big deal."

"You don't look fine. You look like roadkill. You need to get checked out."

But she'd begun to think through the implications. "Except the hospital staff won't thank me for bringing a pack of ravening paps down on the place." Raven grimaced, imagining the photographers harassing doctors, nurses and patients alike for any scrap of gossip, no matter how ridiculous. "Fucking paps. Besides, a trip to the ER isn't necessary. It's just a little headache. I've had worse." She was an old hand at judging how badly she was hurt after two years as Ewan's punching bag.

Kara frowned. "You sure?"

"Yeah." She sighed. "I do want to see Roger, but it's probably best if I stay away."

"Hey, look on the bright side," Monique said, attempting a teasing note that sounded a little forced.

"There's a bright side?"

"Now we know what Nate uses his magic for." She lifted one hand and angled it upward, imitating Nate's flight. "It's a bird... It's a plane... It's a *bodyguard!* Even the cops were impressed."

"Wonder what else he can do with all that Talent?" Kara drawled, a wicked light in her eyes. "Bet he's got some serious *skills*. Talk about magic hands..."

"Would you shut up?" Raven snapped as her cheeks went hot. "You do realize he's standing out in the hall? He can probably hear us." *Though those hands had felt damn good holding her…*

"Good thing you hired him." All humor drained from Monique's face. "If he hadn't been there… Gary would have killed everyone in the building. We all would have died."

"But he *did* save us," Kara said with her usual bracing logic. "No point in worrying about something that didn't happen."

"I think I'm falling in love with him." Raven's eyes flew open as she realized she'd said that out loud.

The two women were staring, but instead of the incredulity she'd expected, they wore matching *No shit* expressions.

Monique snorted. "I could have told you that three months ago."

"Seven," Kara corrected. "Hell, the roadies probably know. Anybody with eyes sees the way you look at him."

Raven winced, wondering if it was that obvious to him too. Probably. Nate was observant as hell. So why hadn't he let on? Was he ignoring her feelings because he didn't share them?

She heaved herself out of the chair. "Let's go home." She sounded exhausted and defeated even to herself. "We'll drop y'all off."

* * *

Nate stood guard in the hall outside the women's dressing room. He felt sick and shaky, a reaction to an adrenaline dump he recognized from past fights. Especially the one with that fucking Iraqi Feral. The Gulf War had barely affected those back home, but it had certainly left its mark on him. *But I'm still better off than the men I didn't manage to save.*

He could already tell today would leave its own scars.

The really infuriating thing was he'd known where this was going. He'd spent the past two weeks watching Handle struggle to learn the basic choreography of the dance number with Raven. The cat spirit had been so agitated by the presence of so many unfamiliar people with so much unfamiliar magic, Gary hadn't been able to concentrate. Nate might have felt sorry for him if the Feral hadn't been such a dick to Raven.

And every time Nate had closed his eyes to look, the cat had gotten closer and closer to taking a bite out of Raven. The whole time he'd watched them in that bed, he'd practiced pouring his magic into his right hand. Knowing his childhood trick might be the only hope they had.

And he'd been right.

Then after he'd managed to take the bastard down -- against all odds -- it had looked like Nate would be going to jail.

Oh, the charges would have been dropped... eventually. Even without the video, a dozen witnesses would have testified he had no choice. After what had happened to Roger, it would be hard for a prosecutor to argue otherwise.

But even a single night in jail would have left Raven without his protection. Bruce was a good bodyguard against most threats, but he was a Norm. He couldn't even see magic, much less use it. Too, Ewan was a Bard. Bards could do a lot more damage than most Norms realized.

Fortunately, Raven's quick thinking about Andy's video had saved Nate from a night in jail -- and herself from something that could have been a hell of a lot worse.

He frowned, remembering Raven's bone-white

face and dazed green eyes. She was going to have trouble with this. It was obvious she thought she'd been a coward by failing to stop Handle. Nate was going to have to convince her to let go of that guilt. Maybe seek therapy, assuming he could talk her into it.

Why do you imagine she'll listen to you? a cynical voice demanded from the back of his head. *You're just muscle. She'd have clung to anybody who saved her from all those teeth. In real life, the good guy doesn't get the girl.*

The dressing room door opened, and Raven emerged in a pair of baggy gray sweats that disguised her lithe figure. What he could see of the pale face under her baseball cap was grim and bare of makeup. She still looked beautiful -- and about fifteen, though he knew she was thirty. Kara and Monique followed, also dressed down until they could have passed for homeless.

"Let's get the hell out of here," she told him.

* * *

When he opened the door to the back service exit, he found a sea of reporters, TV cameras and paparazzi waiting.

Luckily, he'd foreseen the problem and asked the detectives to clear a path so they could get to the limo. Cops hated reporters almost as much as he did, and they'd been happy to help.

Raven grabbed the back of his T-shirt as they headed for the car, moving fast. Bruce Robertson stood by the limo's passenger side, his expression tense as he waited to drive them to safety. He was a solidly muscled man pushing forty, his light brown hair going silver at the temples, the silver stubble of the beard he was trying to grow accentuating the line of his long, square jaw. His dark blue eyes were steady and measuring. Nate had met him in the Marine Corps, where they'd been sergeants in the same platoon, trying to keep their idiot lieutenant alive. When they'd gotten out, Bruce had suggested going into the security business together.

Nights like this, he probably regretted it.

It was hardly the first time he'd had to get Raven through one of these scrums, though the trigger had usually been some ludicrous bit of gossip about who Raven was or was not dating. This situation was a lot more serious, and there was a vicious edge to the questions he'd never heard before.

"Raven! Hey, Raven, is it true you were naked and covered in blood?"

"Raven! Did the Feral eat Roger Timmons?"

"Senator Jessup says all Ferals are demon-possessed and should be executed. Do you think he's right?"

Then to Nate's astonishment, a mic was shoved into *his* face. "Hey, Nate, is it true you killed the Feral? Sources say you used some kind of magic spell. What kinda spell kills Ferals?"

"No comment." Nate shoved the microphone away and gave its owner a stone-cold glare that made the man jolt back a step.

Turning, he scanned the crowd again, looking for an all-too-familiar face. Unfortunately, there were so many people jostling them, so many flashbulbs going off, he couldn't see shit beyond silhouetted figures and strobing glimpses of avid expressions.

Reaching the limo, he guided the women to the rear passenger door Bruce held open. As they piled in, Nate stepped back, again scanning for Ewan.

The cops melted away as Bruce got behind the wheel. Nate shoved his way around the car to the front passenger's side through a forest of microphones and screamed questions.

He wrenched the door open, fighting the impulse to break a camera or two in a blow for human decency. But as he started to slide in, his gaze fell on a lean, pale face across the car roof. A face he recognized despite the black sweatshirt with its hood pulled up. That plus the black sunglasses made the man look like the Unabomber.

Rage blasting through him, Nate slammed the car door and half-dove across the hood of limousine, ignoring the startled yelps of the photographers and reporters.

He didn't give a shit. The paps were about to get pics of Raven's bodyguard beating the living hell out of Ewan Bradley.

Ewan dodged his grab and plunged back into the crowd.

Nate swore, tempted to chase the bastard. Unfortunately, he couldn't leave Bruce to protect Raven by himself. For all he knew, Ewan might double back and shoot into the limo while Nate was chasing shadows.

Cursing steadily, he turned back to the car, grabbed the reporter who'd half-crawled into the passenger seat to question Raven, and tossed him into the crowd. Nate climbed in even as Bruce started the car with a roar.

Evidently recognizing the murder in their eyes, reporters and paps scattered as Bruce gunned the limo and shot off into the night.

Chapter Three

"What the hell was that about?" Raven demanded as Bruce accelerated, taking turns at random to lose the paps.

"Ewan," Nate said grimly. "He was taunting me from the crowd."

"Motherfucker!"

"You know, he doesn't seem quite as terrifying after the whole tiger-tries-to-eat-us thing," Monique said.

"He's terrifying enough." Raven hunched to wrap her arms around herself. "Look, do you guys want to stay at the house tonight?"

"As opposed to being thrown to the paparazzi like a lamb chop to a pack of wolves?" Kara asked dryly. "Hell, yeah, I want to stay at your house."

"The words 'gated community' do have a nice ring right now," Monique agreed.

Nate turned to look over his shoulder out the rear window. They were being followed, but it was a KNBC news van.

As opposed to, say, that candy apple red Porsche 911 Ewan used to get on his last fuckin' nerve. Which was probably why the fucker drove such a noticeable car during his ugly little games. You couldn't terrorize your target if she didn't know it was you.

"You saved our lives back there, Nate," Kara said quietly. "If I haven't said this already... Thank you."

"It is kind of my job," Nate pointed out dryly.

"Your job is to keep an eye out for Ewan," Raven told him. "And he's not anywhere near Gary's weight class. So yeah, you went above and beyond."

Kara snorted. "Ewan ain't exactly harmless. Harmless doesn't give you two concussions, three broken ribs, a broken arm, and more bruises than I can count."

"Getting eaten is still not in Nate's job description."

"I disagree," he said, a bit more sharply than he probably should have. "Besides, Gary would have eaten me anyway."

"Which I could have stopped him from doing if I'd been able to sing. I couldn't even move. It was like I'd been sunk in concrete."

"You weren't the only one," Monique told her. "I couldn't get a note out of my mouth either. And believe me, I tried."

Nate flicked a glance at them in the rear view. He needed to nip this guilt shit in the bud. "You know why I didn't freeze?"

"You have more guts than I do?"

"Six weeks on Parris Island having sadistic drill sergeants shoot live ordinance off over my head. Besides, singing wouldn't have done a damn bit of good anyway. It takes time to sing someone under a spell, and Handle was on Roger in a fraction of a second."

Nate glanced back at the three women. One look at Raven's face told him he wasn't getting through. *It's like playing darts with a concrete wall. Nothing's going to stick.*

He sighed and turned to keep an eye on the road in case Ewan took another run at them.

"So what the hell happened back there?" Bruce asked, glancing over at him. "You were a little skimpy on the details."

"You should have seen him, Bruce," Monique said before Nate could reply. "He hit Fur Boy like an eighteen wheeler. It was a thing of beauty."

The women took turns telling the story in such glowing terms that Nate felt uncomfortable.

Bruce shot him a look. "So the Fist actually worked, huh?" He shook his head. "I'll be damned."

"The fist?" Raven asked, sounding intrigued. "What's the fist?"

Bruce grinned at them in the rearview mirror. "Our boy here was a comic book geek back in the day…"

"Jesus, Bruce, give me a break," Nate groaned.

His friend just smirked and continued. "So there was this martial artist in one of Nate's favorite comics who had the ability to focus all his magic or chi or some shit into one fist…"

Deciding he'd better take control of the story before his friend revealed something really embarrassing, Nate interrupted. "Since I was about ten at the time, I started wondering if I could use my Primo Talent to do the same thing. Turns out I could." He grimaced. "And being a ten-year-old idiot, I proceeded to smash my fist through a concrete block. Good news is, it worked. Bad news is, I broke my hand. So I taught myself how to build a protective magical shield around my fist. Otherwise I'd have broken every bone in my arm when I hit Gary's manifestation. Punching a Tooth Tank isn't a good idea."

Raven's brows lifted. "So you make a habit of putting your fist through armor plating?"

"Nope, but he did win a bet by punching through a car door once," Bruce said, slanting him an evil grin.

"How drunk were you?" Kara asked dryly.

Bruce cackled. "Boy had downed enough Scotch to float a battleship off a sand bar."

"I did not!" He paused to smirk. "It was a Coast Guard Cutter, tops."

Before they could quit laughing long enough to ask any more embarrassing questions, the mobile phone started ringing. Over the rest of the trip home, everyone from Raven's agent to the CEO of Bard Records called to make sure she was still breathing.

The Bard CEO said Roger's wife had told him the director was in surgery, probably the first of many operations. The surgeon had said it didn't look good for his arm, but Roger would probably survive, thanks to Nate's tourniquet.

The news about the director's arm left the group silent and grim the rest of the way home.

* * *

Raven's Spanish Colonial-style mansion lay in a gated community perched on the hillside not far from Runyon Canyon. Two stories of cream stucco walls and red tile roof, the sprawling house boasted ten bedrooms, a pool, a recording studio, and a private screening room. She adored the place, with its big, airy rooms and the art nouveau furnishings she'd collected since making it big. You couldn't beat the gorgeous view of Los Angeles either, though Raven knew Nate had nightmares of Ewan drawing a bead on her through one of the huge arched windows.

Bruce drove through the security gate set in the ten-foot wall she'd had erected after Ewan's first little visit. But as they started up the winding drive to the garage, Nate told him to stop. "Stay with the ladies, please. I need to clear the house and grounds." As his partner complied, he flexed his big fists. "Maybe Ewan's here and I'll get to beat the bastard to death. I've had about enough of him."

Bruce eyed him. "Haven't you bagged your

asshole limit for the night?"

"Nope." Nate drew his gun and slid out into the darkness.

"You," Monique said to Raven, "are a lucky, lucky bitch." She fanned her face with a long-nailed hand and laughed.

Raven didn't. And as long moments slid back without him reappearing, her tension grew. *What if Ewan is here? What if he ambushes Nate?* "Shouldn't you back him up?" she asked Bruce.

"Nope," the big man told her placidly. "You don't leave the client alone."

"But what if…"

He gave her a long look in the rearview mirror. "As he just demonstrated today, Nate can take care of himself."

She huffed out a breath in frustration. "You don't know Ewan like I do."

Kara took her hand, her grip warm and comforting. "He probably isn't even here. Ewan's not going want to go up against these two." She curled her upper lip. "The cowardly little creep prefers opponents he outweighs."

Monique began to hum, her voice soft and potent with magic, and between the two of them, Raven felt her tension drain.

A few minutes later, the garage door hummed up and Nate gestured for Bruce to drive in. He parked next to Raven's Jag and Nate's Camry, and they all trooped through the kitchen entrance.

Just walking through the door made Raven's knotted back muscles begin to relax for the first time in hours. Blowing out a breath, she rolled her shoulders in relief.

The kitchen had become her sanctuary between

tours and recording. Preparing gourmet meals was a soothing reminder she no longer had to live on ramen and peanut butter sandwiches.

Instead of a hotplate and tiny fridge, she owned a kitchen full of high-end equipment, including a hulking Viking range and a huge built-in Sub-Zero refrigerator. There was an acre of marble prep surfaces where she could create any damn thing she wanted. The maple cabinetry had frosted glass doors scrolled with vines and flowers. Hanging baskets of growing herbs hung beside the windows over the long sink, scenting the air with rosemary, sage, oregano and dill.

Not that she had the wherewithal to boil an egg at the moment. But still.

With a sigh, Raven headed for the refrigerator to grab several bottles of *PowerUp*, a combo energy drink/potion designed to recharge magical batteries and fight migraines. When she handed them out, even Nate took one. He must be nursing his own backlash headache from punching Gary's manifestation.

Usually her friends could be counted for laugher and teasing, but tonight everyone was too damned tired. Bruce called his wife to pick him up, while Monique and Kara headed to their respective guest rooms. Raven headed for her own, leaving the two men to their strategizing about what to do if Ewan showed up again.

Until a year ago, she'd thought the bastard was out of her life for good. Then the *Rolling Stone* article hit, and he'd broken in a night later. Fortunately, Kara had been there at the time, and he'd fled when the women met him at the broken window with guns drawn.

They'd hired Nate's company the next day.

Robertson and Carter Security was a small,

brand-new firm, but that had been a big part of its appeal. Ewan had far too many connections with local law enforcement through his father, a federal judge, and most of the other security firms employed former cops. R&C seemed a lot less likely to look the other way if Ewan decided to try something.

Raven climbed the wrought-iron spiral staircase that led to her floor, with its office, recording studio, and her suite. Nate's rooms were right across the hall, a fact she found even more comforting than usual tonight.

Thinking of him helped her dredge up the energy to change into one of the ankle-length silk nightgowns that made her feel like a film noir heroine. Before Nate had moved in, she slept in oversized concert tees.

She felt face-first across the bed and was asleep ten seconds later.

* * *

The glowing tiger leaped at her, roaring, clawed paws spread wide.

This time Nate wasn't there.

"Raven!" Nate shouted through the door. "Raven, open the door or I'm breaking it down!"

The urgency in his voice dragged her from the depth of the nightmare. "Coming!" Confused, shaking, Raven rolled out of bed and staggered to the door to open it.

Nate stood on the other side, wearing only a pair of jeans. The Ruger was in his hand. "What happened?" His muscled body tense, he pushed past her, scanning the bedroom, then moving fast to check the walk-in closets, the bathroom, even beneath the bed. Satisfied, he stood to join her again after turning out the lights he'd turned on. They stood there a moment, studying each other in the dim green glow of one Tiffany lamp and the moonlight streaming silver through the heavy gold curtains. "Why'd you scream?"

Raven stared at him, confused. The last shreds of the nightmare vanished, leaving a fuzzy impression of intense terror. She rolled her shoulders, trying to shrug it off. "I screamed?"

"Yeah. I thought it was Ewan."

"No, it was just a nightmare. I think." She winced and raked both hands through her hair, embarrassed. "I'm sorry I woke you."

His broad shoulders relaxed, and he nodded, turning toward the door.

Raven realized she desperately did not want him to leave. "Could you... Could you sit with me a minute? I know it's late but... It was a *really* bad dream." She felt like an idiot, but she wasn't quite proud enough to let him leave.

"Of course," he said, and put the safety on the Ruger.

Raven groped for something socially acceptable they could do. She longed to ask him to sleep with her -- *just* sleep -- but she didn't quite have the guts. Her gaze fell on the gold couch that stood on the opposite side of the room from the bed. It was positioned in front of the fireplace, a small round end table beside it. "Let's go sit down."

Nate followed her and set his weapon down on the little table, next to her very first Grammy, a Tiffany lamp, and a couple of books. He looked up at her as she hesitated, not sure this was a good idea. His face softened and he caught her wrist, pulling her down beside him. To her surprise, he slid an arm around her shoulders.

He felt delightfully warm. Strong. Raven sighed

and relaxed against him, letting her head rest against his bare, muscled shoulder. She glanced sideways, wanting to purr in pleasure. His chest was all sculpted muscle, with a ruff of dark hair that looked soft, making her long to touch. His big feet were bare, and he sat with his legs apart, drawing her gaze to the line of his zipper.

Was he getting hard?

The last of the dream's fear residue slid away, banished by the first warm rise of desire. Their eyes met, and heat flared in his gaze. She swallowed. "Um, hi."

"Hi, yourself." Nate shifted and looked around as if groping for a safe topic of conversation. His eyes fell on her bed and quickly rose, locking on the painting that hung over it. "Is that your mom?"

She followed his gaze. Raven had been about twelve, dressed in a red corduroy jumper, her hair in pigtails, leaning into her mother's shoulder. Mom had looked so damn much like Raven herself now -- the same green eyes and pointed chin, hair the same shade of blonde, though her mother had worn it in a shoulder-length cascade of curls. Mom had looked so young, so happy, so sure she'd find the stardom her Bard brilliance promised...

Raven cleared her throat against the sudden ache. "Yeah. I commissioned it from one of those Sears studio photographs."

Nate smiled. "I remember those. We had one of the whole family. Mom, Dad, us three boys." He studied the painting thoughtfully. "She looks a lot like you. Was she a Bard too?" Talent ran in families, but it wasn't unknown for parents with different gifts to marry.

"Yeah," Raven said. "She was good too. I think

she could have been a star if she'd ever caught a break. But she was always too busy trying to keep me in food and clothes to chase her own dreams."

"What about your dad?"

"He walked out. My father had no intention of giving up *his* dreams, though he didn't manage stardom either." Raven huffed. "He actually contacted me a couple of years ago, trying to talk me into doing a duet with him."

Nate blinked. "That took balls."

"Especially considering what happened when Mom got killed."

He frowned as if searching his memory. "It was a drunk driver, right? You did those PSAs…"

Raven nodded, remembering the shock and horror of the coroner's call. "He ran over her as she was walking home from work. I was fifteen. The social worker tracked Dad down, but he wasn't interested in taking me in. Luckily, Kara's folks *were* willing, or I'd have had to go into foster care. We'd been best friends since kindergarten."

Nate lifted a brow at her. "So when Daddy asked you to do that duet…"

"… I told him to fuck right off." She shook her head. "Mom had to work multiple jobs because he wouldn't give us a dime. She never complained. Never blamed me for what she hadn't been able to do because of me."

Raven glanced around the room, smiling a little. "She would've loved this house." Reminded, she pushed aside the paperback she'd been reading and picked up a worn, battered oversized hardback called *The Artistry of Art Nouveau* and flipped open the well-thumbed pages. "Mom found this in a used bookstore when I was a kid. We'd sit and look at the pictures, and she'd talk about the mansion she'd build when she became a star. So when I bought this place, I decorated it just like that." She turned pages until she found a picture of a brass bed with a towering head and footboard, its metal bars curled in the shapes of flowering vines.

Nate leaned close to look over her shoulder. His brows rose as he looked up at the bed with its tumbled emerald comforter bordered in gold honeysuckle. "Isn't that your bed?"

"Not quite." She smiled a little. "I couldn't find that one, though I did look. So I commissioned a brass sculptor to replicate it."

"I always wondered about this place," he murmured. "The other stars we've visited -- they decorate in either pricey antiques or steel and glass. Demonstrating their money and taste, the things they can afford. I'm not surprised you'd decorate for love."

She blinked at his perception. "Yeah. I guess I do."

Their eyes met. There was hunger in his gaze, a need and longing that mirrored her own. His lips parted, and his tongue slipped out, tasting his lower lip as if imagining kissing her.

He wants me. Raven's breathing grew rougher, and her gaze slid helplessly down to his lap, almost against her will. She caught her breath.

He had an erection. It bulked hard against his zipper, thick and promising. It was her turn to lick dry lips. Her heart began to pound. *He* wants *me. I thought he didn't feel anything, but he does.*

Nate swallowed and stirred uneasily, then rose abruptly to his feet. "I'd better get back to my room..."

"Don't go." She was on her feet before she could think better of it. "I... need you." It was the most naked admission she'd ever made in her life. Before she could think better of it, she stepped in close, wrapping both arms around his strong neck as she rose on her toes. And kissed him with all the tortured hunger she'd been trying to ignore for months.

Nate froze, his lips unmoving against hers.

Her stomach plummeted. Raven let her bare heels drop and stepped back. "I'm sorry. I'm sorry. I shouldn't have..." Blindly, she spun and started for the door, wanting only to get away. Never mind this was her room -- she couldn't stay here. Not with pain stabbing into her chest like a razor-honed stiletto.

"Raven." The deep, rough note in his voice stopped her. She hesitated, caught between turning to him and running away...

Nate's hands closed around her shoulders, spun her around and pulled her in close. Against the erection she could feel against her stomach like a length of pipe. His eyes met hers, hungry, almost desperate. "I shouldn't do this. *We* shouldn't do this. It's not a good idea. It's going to make this job a lot more complicated."

Her mouth went dry. "I know. I just can't seem to care." She swallowed, looking up at that fierce, handsome face. She rose on her toes, wanting to taste him again... And stopped. This time the kiss needed to be his idea. "Or maybe I care too much. *Want* too much."

"God, yes." And his mouth was on hers in a kiss hot with all the hunger she'd ever dreamed of. All the hunger she'd never known from any man she'd cared about. Especially not Ewan.

It was an erotic explosion of a kiss, hot and passionate and desperately needy, his tongue stroking in and out of her mouth in a slick duel with her own.

She tasted mint toothpaste and Nate, drank in the clean male scent, intoxicating and overwhelming.

Until she pulled back just far enough to breathe. "I need not to think. Every time I close my eyes, I keep seeing Roger. Keep seeing that fucking tiger..."

"Then I'll have to keep you from thinking," Nate murmured, so rough and low her nipples peaked.

Staring up into his handsome face, Raven couldn't believe she was finally in his arms. Finally feeling the heat and hardness of him, the rock steadiness of his arms. "Maybe neither one of us should think for a while." She stepped back and caught his wrist, backing toward the bed. He scooped up the gun off the end table as he followed. Bodyguard to the core.

Raven's heart hammered in her chest. Hungry to touch him before he changed his mind and backed off into that frustrating distance he'd maintained between them.

The thought that he might want to retreat made her break step despite her body's outraged howl of protest. Anxiously, she examined his face in the moonlight coming through the curtains. "You *do* want me, right? I'm not... This isn't... I know I'm your boss, and..."

"No, this isn't sexual harassment." Nate smiled down at her in genuine amusement, gaze absorbed as he studied her face as if committing it to memory. "I've wanted you for months. But..." He shrugged.

"Are you sure? There was this big shot Bard Records executive once who didn't want to take no for an answer and I..."

Nate's eyes narrowed and cooled. "What's this asshole's name? I'd be happy to pay him a visit." And judging by the glitter of his eyes, it wouldn't be one the jerk enjoyed.

"He got fired." They reached the bed and Nate put the gun down on the nightstand in easy reach. "It was a condition of me signing with Bard. Normally I wouldn't set out to get somebody canned, but that jerk had been harassing women for years." She brushed her fingers over the hair on his chest, feeling the springy texture over the warm, velvet flesh, the tight plates of muscle. "Being a 'star' is good for some things, anyway."

"You're good for one hell of a lot," Nate rumbled, and dipped his head to kiss her again, one big, warm hand cupping her cheek.

Raven had touched him before during the self-defense lessons he'd given her. But she'd never *touched* him. Never tested the sensitivity of tight male nipples, felt him draw in a hungry breath. Now she could lean in and trace the lean tendons in his throat with her tongue, kiss his Adam's apple, run her hand down his chest to explore the intriguing territory of his abdominals. He wasn't some steroid-pumped gym rat -- he was leaner, more martial artist than heavyweight boxer.

And as he'd proven today, he was also far more deadly than either.

She leaned in and kissed his chest, just to the right of one hard nipple. Bit gently at the hard muscle of his pec and listened to his indrawn breath.

Unable to resist, she angled her head back to check his reaction.

His eyes met hers, his lips quirking in a dark and sexy smile. He brushed a forefinger over the rise of her cheek as Raven gazed up into his eyes, pewter in the moonlight. He sought out the hollow of her collarbone with that finger, brushed across the upper curves of her breast. Dipped teasingly, making her think he was about to delve into the bodice of her nightgown.

Instead his hand veered away, sliding down her body to curve around her ribcage. "I really like your gown," he said in a voice that rasped with hunger. "But I think I'd like it even better off you."

"And I like your..." She found the waistband of his jeans and toyed with the snap. His erection pulled the fabric tight, a silent testament to his hunger. "...*Everything.*"

He grinned. "And my everything likes you right back."

She flicked the snap open. "But I am getting a little... impatient."

"Well, we can't have that." And he cupped her breast though the silk. Raven gasped as her entire body seemed to burst into flames. She swallowed, and cupped him in turn through the tight dark denim, feeling the promise of his furiously erect cock. Raven shivered, imagining how it would feel sliding into her. Felt her pussy go even more slick and swollen. Raven flicked the snap open, tugged the tab of the zipper down, then slid her hand into his open fly. She touched hot, bare skin and felt the broad shaft spill into her hand. "Commando?" she breathed against his lips.

His mouth curved. "I almost charged across the hall buck naked."

"Mmmm." An image flashed through her mind -- Nate, bursting in gloriously nude, gun in hand. "Well, that would have gotten things going a lot faster." She hummed in delight at the way his cock filled her fingers. His skin was deliciously warm, soft over his shaft's hard core. Her thumb brushed over the velvet tip, discovered a tiny drop of precum. Scooped it up, and unable to resist, she popped her finger into her mouth.

Nate's eyes went wide, his lips parting. Then he swooped down, pushing her back down on the bed onto her back, and then dragging down her bodice to expose one nipple. His mouth closed over it in rough hunger as his body pressed her down. Hard, deliciously heavy. Deliciously male.

Raven caught her breath at the sweet, silvery pleasure of his swirling tongue, then gasped as his teeth closed gently over the point, raking, pulling, teasing her with a lush cascade of sensation.

Her eyes drifted closed as he feasted on each nipple in turn. As her grip tightened on his cock, he growled and suckled harder, making her shiver. Her free hand slid up to the nape of his neck, long nails raking gently over the sensitive skin.

Through her closed eyes, she saw his magic burning like a torch, pulsing brighter with every pounding heartbeat.

When she opened her eyes, he was staring into her face, nose flaring as if drinking in her scent. He swallowed. "I think this very pretty nightgown needs to come off."

Her gaze dropped to his open fly, and she licked her lips again. "So do those jeans."

"I think we can do that." His lips twitched and he straightened off the bed with a glorious roll of his muscled body. She watched hungrily as he slid his jeans down his thighs, revealing the rest of that glorious warrior's body, the thick cock dancing as he moved.

She sat up to reach for the hem of nightgown, tugging it out from beneath her body. Nate leaned in to gather up fistfuls of skirt, pull it off over her head, and toss it across the room.

For moment, they stared at each other. Her heart pounded a thick, hot beat as she looked down at his cock -- its long, elegant shape, the head a bit narrower than the thick shaft, balls surrounded by soft, dark hair. Moonlight painted his muscled body in silver and shadow.

Yes, he wants me. But does he love me? Because I think I love him. Raven shut the thought down hard. She wanted to concentrate on this moment. *Needed* to.

Raven lay back on the bed as he eased down on top of her, all muscle and heat, supporting himself on his elbows. Making her feel safe, truly safe in the way only he could since Ewan had invaded her peace.

Their mouths met again in heat and urgency, lips pressing, hers opening wide for his tongue as it stroked hers with swirling skill. His big hands slid through her short-cropped hair. He drew back a moment, staring down into her eyes, his own gray ones looking dark, flecked with reflections from the window. His lips were parted, a little damp. His tongue flicked out, tracing his lower lip. "God, you're beautiful. So…"

"You… you too." And winced. *Oh, for God's sake. You're a singer-song writer. Is that the best you can come up with?*

Given how little blood was making it to her brain, probably.

Nate leaned in and started kissing his way down her chin, teeth grazing her jaw, then sliding lower, to the pulse jumping in her throat.

She wrapped her arms around him, losing herself in the contours and weight of his hard body, tracing the contours of his broad back, savoring the heat of his skin.

He cupped her bare breast, thumb flicking the erect nipple. His touch felt so delicious, she shivered in pleasure and caressed him back, exploring the tight flesh over his ribs, the ripple of hard abdominal muscles. She could feel the jut of his cock against her belly, thick and promising.

Spreading her other hand across his shoulders, she explored the thick, hard muscle. Felt a round, puckered scar high on his chest. It could have only come from a bullet. Raven made a soft purr of sympathy. Found a tight male nipple and stroked it with her thumb. He rewarded her with a throaty rumble. She slid one hand down the tight curve of his biceps and found a set of ridges curving around it. More scars. Too regular to be shrapnel...

Raven remembered the deep slashes in Roger's arm where the tiger had gripped him, bitten him. Remembered Nate talking about the Iraqi Feral who'd attacked his unit.

Nate had known firsthand what a Feral could do, but he'd attacked Gary anyway.

To save her. Save them all.

"Hey." His voice was low but determined. Demanding. "Concentrate on now. Not what happened years ago. I'm fine."

She blinked. "How did you know...?"

"You touched the scars, and I felt you stiffen. Not hard to figure out you'd put two and two together." His voice took on a teasing note as his eyes gleamed wickedly. "It's also obvious I need to give you something more interesting to think about. Better yet, I need to make it impossible for you to think at all." Lowering his head, he closed his velvet lips over her nipple and sucked it into his mouth again. The wet delight bowed her back off the mattress. She closed her eyes at the raw pleasure of it all.

In the darkness, his hands burned like torches, as

though he poured his Primo magic into her.

Seemed he could do a lot more with his Talent than kill psychotic Ferals. No wonder his every touch felt so much more intense than anything she'd ever experienced.

Raven had heard of Primos using their magic this way, but she'd never had a lover who could do it. Breath caught, she watched those magic hands play, teasing her nerve endings with exquisite little brushes and curls of magic.

So damned good...

* * *

This is a very bad idea, the voice of sanity told Nate.

Fuck off. This might be the only chance he'd ever have to love Raven. To do the things he'd been dreaming about since he'd met her. She'd be on to the next boy toy in a week, maybe two.

But she was damn well going to remember him when it was over. She was going to associate him with something more than blood and terror and misplaced gratitude with a side order of hero worship.

He lifted his head to check her face for the effect he was having. Those green eyes were closed, her expression rapt, as if watching the play of magic around them. Her breasts felt deliciously full in his hands, the nipples exquisitely responsive as he tugged and squeezed. Concentrating fiercely on the pleasure he wanted her to feel, Nate let more sparks of power trail from his fingertips, teasing her into the pleasure he wanted to inspire. "I want my mouth on you," he told her, voice so low and rough it growled.

"Me... me too," she gasped. "I want... want you to feel good too!"

He grinned. "Oh, believe me, I'm feeling very,

very good."

How often had he seen her dance on stage, her voice pouring magic over the crowd, her sensual dancing casting spells even without a Primo's magic? Those incredible legs, that lithe body with just enough seductive jiggle to make every man in the audience get glaze-eyed...

How many times had he been forced to retreat into the deepest backstage shadows to hide his erection?

Now he felt that exquisite body roll under his hands as he worked his way lower to the treasure between those long, long legs. He couldn't wait to taste her pussy. He could smell how wet she was already. When he slid a hand between her lips, she was as deliciously slick and ready as he'd hoped. His cock bucked in anticipation as he slipped a finger inside. *God, she's tight.*

Starved for the taste of her, he started to slide between her legs. He wanted to tongue her there. Taste all that luscious juice.

"My turn!"

Nate froze as her power whipped over him.

"Over on your back," she gasped.

He flipped over, totally unable to resist her Bard magic. Not that he really wanted to, but still.

Raven swung one leg astride his hips and looked down at him with glittering eyes. "Now," she purred. "What am I going to do with you?"

"No... no fair," he managed.

For moment she looked a little shamefaced at using her magic on him. "I just have to touch you. I've wanted to touch you for months."

"What a coincidence. Same goes."

But she didn't appear to hear as she stroked long

fingers over the contours and ridges of his body, even the scars that had gone keloid and ugly. Raven kissed the bullet wound, the old claw scars. Kissed them as if she wished she could heal them.

Apparently she didn't realize that her touch alone did that.

Her delicate fingers wrapped around his cock again, slid down to his balls, weighed and caressed them. Bending over him, she began to work her way down, licking along the ripple of ribs and abdominal muscles toward that eager, bobbing cock.

"Sixty-nine?" He was all but begging and didn't care. "I want that hot little pussy."

Her eyes flashed up at him, and she gave him a wicked little grin. "Well, if you insist."

She rose, turned her back, and presented him with her exquisite ass. He groaned and reached to part her. Stroked his thumb between the lips, found her clit. Curled up to eat her, tongue lapping up all that glorious cream, tasting clean woman and arousal and a hint of mango soap.

Her mouth engulfed the head of his cock, and Nate's eyes almost crossed. He groaned against her flesh as one delicate hand gripped him hard, the other cupping his balls. He stroked his thumb around her clit and fought to concentrate on eating her, suckling that deliciously wet flesh.

"Nate!" She threw her head back with a startled shout, and he closed his eyes to watch the magic of her climax roll through her aura. *She's definitely not faking* that.

Then her mouth closed tight around his cock, and she sucked him down deep and hard. And began to hum, the seductive vibrations of her throat and lips reverberating through his own aura.

He shuddered helplessly as an orgasm began to build, that amazing Talent of hers finding every nerve in his cock and making them fire like a battleship's guns. He fought not to come with a desperation that grew increasingly ragged. "Oh, Jesus, stop!" he begged as his control slipped. "Or this is gonna be over way too fast!"

Raven released his cock with a juicy pop of her lips. "Then I guess you'll have to concentrate on keeping it together," she said, wicked humor in her voice. Then she took him into her mouth and hummed again.

Her magic had released its grip, and he could move now. He was damned if he was going to miss his chance. "Condom!" he growled. "I'm clean, but only an idiot has sex without a condom." Not with HIV raging and no cure in sight.

"Nightstand drawer," she said. To his pleasure, she sounded just as desperate as he felt.

He reached to pull it open one-handed, fished around until he found a foil square. Raven took it and rolled it onto his shaft, slowly -- so slooowly -- her gaze absorbed, her color flushed, green eyes glittering. He had to clench his fists and fight his own overstimulated body.

When she had him sheathed at last, she swung a leg astride him and rose onto her knees. Her green gaze locked on his face as she angled his cock upward and took him deep and slow. The tight, sucking heat of her grip damn near tipped him right over, but he fought it down again with all the discipline he'd ever learned as his father's son.

Nate reached up, cupped her breast in one hand, began to tease the tight pink nipple as he stared into those exquisite eyes.

They widened, went vague as she sank lower, lower, her lips parting until her lush ass rested over his balls. "You... you fill me. Up."

"Yeah," he rasped. "Yeah, you fill me up too. With your magic. With you." He reached between them with his other hand, found her clit with his thumb. And sent a hot little curl of magic dancing over the tiny nub.

Raven shuddered and groaned, then began to push slowly up his shaft. The sensation of that impossibly wet cunt gripping him made him grateful for the condom. Otherwise he doubted he'd be able to hold on.

But she was damn well going to go over *with* him. He poured more magic into his hands, gathering the pleasure coiling in his balls, in his cock, glorying in her tight, slick heat. Feeding it back to her as she stroked up and down.

Rising. Falling. Slowly at first, almost lazily. Then faster. Pumping until he had to work to keep his hands in place on her breast and her clit.

He listened to her ragged gasps as she rode him. Rolling his hips, he flooded magic into his cock and she yowled, screaming in the raw delight of her second climax.

Discipline deserted him, and he began to grind, burying himself to the balls in all her creamy heat. Again. Again. Again.

Raven matched his rhythm with her dancer's skill as he fed her pussy still more magic with every rock of his hips as she began to chant his name. Spilling power into the word, almost singing it until he came so hard magic exploded around them in a rain of sparks and passion.

He'd never come that hard in his life.

With one last long cry, she collapsed on top on top of him, both arms flung around his shoulders as he wrapped himself around her.

Panting and sweating and sated. At least for the moment.

Chapter Four

Raven fell into an exhausted sleep, her head pillowed on Nate's chest. He curled his arms around her, loving the feel of that soft, slender body curled into his, the full breasts cuddled against his chest. Those little nipples had tasted so sweet.

A smile curved his mouth, and he stroked one hand up and down her slender, silken back.

A thought flitted through his mind. *The guys in my platoon would never believe I slept with Raven Garland.* Somebody had played one of her CDs damn near every night during the war.

Not that he was going to tell them. Honor might be an old-fashioned concept, but it was one his dad had drilled into their heads from the time they could walk.

Thinking of his father, Nate winced. His parents would be appalled if they'd known he'd fallen for Raven. But though he loved and respected them, they didn't get to dictate his life anymore.

Besides, it wasn't like this relationship was going anywhere. They generally didn't with her. Probably because of that fucker Ewan and her hellish marriage. Anybody would be gun shy after that.

In the months Nate had been her bodyguard, he'd seen her fall in love twice, once with a Primo dancer, then with a pretty-boy actor with more muscle than brains. Both affairs had flamed out fast.

No surprise, since each man had been using her. The Primo had wanted her money, while the actor's career had flatlined. He'd needed the buzz of an affair with Raven Garland to resuscitate it.

The puzzling thing was why Raven had played along with either prick. Men often took one look at that lovely face and tempting body and never noticed the razor keen intelligence that came with the package. So she'd known what the himbos were after.

He remembered the look he'd seen on her face in the rearview mirror when he was driving her and her dates around. Her fun-loving grin had been belied by the sadness in her eyes.

He suspected she viewed partying as another part of the entertainment she provided her fans. The himbos were part of the act.

She deserved better. Nate would love to be that "better." Yet sweet as this was, it wasn't going to go anywhere. At least, not on her end. His feelings, unfortunately, were an entirely different matter.

He was in love with Raven Garland.

And she was dealing with guilt and gratitude and maybe a little hero worship, none of which were going to last.

He didn't think he could take being another one of her empty flings. He was already in love with her. If she ran true to her pattern, he was going to end up with his heart shredded like pulled pork.

He needed to rebuild that professional distance between them.

So what the hell are you doing in bed with her? asked a sardonic mental voice. *You're just asking for it.* He eyed her exhausted face, wondering if there was any way he could slip out of her bed without waking her.

But that would be a dick move. It would imply she was just a piece of ass, which she wasn't and never would be as far as he was concerned. After what her ex had done to her, it wasn't even an option. Yet he had no desire to feed his heart into a shredder either. He just wasn't...

Raven moaned -- and it wasn't a sound of

pleasure. "No," she groaned, stirring against him. "No, Gary... Don't... Nate!" Her voice rose on the last word, sharp with pain and terror.

Oh, shit. "It's all right," Nate whispered, laying a gentle hand on her shoulder. "You're okay. Gary's dead. You're safe. I'm safe. Everything's fine." *If you don't count the armless director and the pack of paparazzi outside the gate.*

She sucked in a gasp of terror, and Nate winced. He hesitated a moment, then tightened his hold and raised his voice. "Raven, wake up."

She jerked, and her eyes flew open. Realizing she was in someone's arms, Raven drew breath to scream.

"It's me!" He fought to keep his tone calm and level. "It's Nate."

Awareness flitted in her eyes, and Raven huddled back into his arms. "Oh, God, I dreamed he'd killed you." She was shaking, racking waves of shivering as her nails dug into his skin. "You were dead. He'd killed you..."

"But he *didn't*. I'm safe. You're safe. It's all good."

Raven lifted her head and looked at him, and his heart sank at the gratitude on her face. Then she shifted in his arms and began to kiss him, her mouth desperate, almost ferocious with relief.

She reached down the length of his body and wrapped one of those long-fingered hands around his cock. Which, damn it, proceeded to get stone hard from the sheer hunger in her kiss.

Bad idea, Nate, warned the cool instincts that used to warn him when he was walking into an ambush.

"Make love to me again," Raven begged, her voice hoarse. "You really do have magic hands." She gave him a smile, but it looked a little too tight, as if it lay over hysteria like a skim of ice over Lake Michigan.

"I'm... not sure that's such a good idea," he managed.

She rocked back and stared at him, hurt in her eyes. *Shit*. He felt like six kinds of asshole, but he knew perfectly well that if he made love to her again, he was well and truly fucked. In all senses of the phrase.

"Why not? I'm on the pill. I've been tested, and I'm clean..."

"That's not it. Look, sleeping with clients is unprofessional as hell and I shouldn't have done it. I got carried away."

She stared at him. "Unprofessional?"

The wounded tone made him wince. "My job is making sure that asshole Ewan doesn't get you." He stroked his fingertips over the high curving rise of her cheekbone. "If I'm obsessing over you, thinking about the last time I made love to you, dreaming of the next time I *will* make love to you, my full attention won't be on my job. I can't take that kind of chance with your life."

"I don't care. I need you," she said, the pleading in the words naked. "Nate, I'm in love with you."

He stared, fighting the rise of incredulous joy. "What?"

She swallowed. "I'm... I'm in love with you. Have been falling for you for months. The girls have been kidding me about it." Raven winced a little. "Monique says even the roadies know."

God, he wanted to believe her. Wanted to believe that his aching heart had a chance.

Unfortunately, he knew otherwise. Women like Raven did not fall for men like him -- military brats with scarred bodies and haunted, guilty minds who'd done and seen a little too much. "Look, having a brush with death like that, it cracks you wide open. Just blows all your shields away and makes you feel things that aren't real."

She stared at him with the first sparks of anger in her eyes. "I'm not a kid, Nate. I've been married. I know what I'm feeling."

"Do you?" Cornered, feeling desperate, he demanded, "What's this -- the third time you've fallen in love this year?"

She stared at him as if he'd slapped her. To his horror, her eyes went glassy and a tear spilled down her cheek, perfect and gleaming in the moonlight. "You bastard."

He wanted to take it back. "I'm sorry, Raven, I didn't mean that."

"Get out."

So he rolled out of bed and did. He should have been relieved at the escape, but it hurt too fucking much.

* * *

Raven snarled at the door he'd closed behind him. "Asshole."

What did you expect? Another relationship self-destructs. Maybe the problem isn't them -- it's you. The snide mental voice sounded a fuck of a lot like Ewan.

Before she could spin off into another soul-searing memory of Raven Garland's Greatest Shits, the phone rang. She plucked the handset off the base. Kara was screening her calls, and if she'd let one through, Raven needed to take it.

Sure enough, the caller ID read Ron Myers.

Raven sighed. Ron had been her manager for the past eight years, and she considered him more or less a friend, but he could be a dick. *I've had entirely too much dick tonight as it is.* "Hi, Ron."

"*LA Morning* wants to interview you and Nate at 7:43 a.m., along with whoever else was there."

She grimaced. "Ron, damn it, I am not going to profit off this fucking tragedy."

"No, but you *are* going to get ahead of this fucking *scandal*," he snapped back. "Like it or not, Roger is going to end up missing an arm and your bodyguard shot that asshole Feral. Handle's parents are saying you're at fault. They're planning to sue."

She dropped back against the headboard with a tired sigh. "Maybe they have a point. If I'd been able to sing him down…"

"Raven, he tried to *eat* you. You aren't the one at fault." He paused. "But there's a bigger problem. Your prick ex has been spinning lies to every reporter who will listen. I think he's trying to get you charged with felony magic."

She straightened in alarm. "God, what's he saying now?"

"That Roger pissed you off, and you used your voice to drive Handle insane so he'd tear into the poor bastard."

Her jaw dropped. "And they're *buying* that? I have a restraining order on the son of a bitch. Did it not occur to them that he's making it up?"

"Of course, they realize he's probably making it up. They also figure it will be good TV to have both of you on."

Raven's eyes widened as her heart began to pound with dread. "Wait, what? No. No, I'm not getting anywhere near that psycho. I didn't get that restraining order for giggles, Ron. And I have the X-rays to prove it."

"Yeah, I told the show's booker as much. She says they've scheduled him for seven sharp and swears they'll have him out of the building before you arrive."

"Nate's not gonna like this."

"Hell, I don't like it either, but we've got to get you out in front of this. Spike Ewan's guns."

Fury blew through the fear. "You call my lawyer *now*. Have him tell Ewan I'm going to release every single photo and every single X-ray if he tries this crap with me. I will tell the entire Goddamn world he beat me the whole two years we were married. Let's see what that does for his precious career. I'm a hell of a lot better liked he is."

He snorted. "That ain't hard. Everybody who knows that prick considers him an asshole. To everyone else, he's just a one hit-wonder whose only claim to fame is that he used to be married to you."

"And as for his accusations, there's video that makes clear I didn't sing a word. This will blow back on Ewan a lot harder than on me."

"Not that I don't approve of the idea, but the judge..." Ron began uneasily.

"The judge raised a sociopath... and the apple didn't fall far from the tree. If His Honor doesn't want a shitload of very bad publicity, he'd better shut his spawn up. I kept quiet about Ewan because of that bastard, but I'm tired of being bullied. I *will* cut loose on both of them -- and I am not a helpless twenty-year-old nobody anymore. I can rain so much fire down on Samuel Bradley, he'll think he's hit hell ahead of schedule."

Ron sighed. "Yeah, okay. I'll get on the phone to the lawyer now. 'Night."

"'Night." Resisting the urge to slam the phone down, she hung up and fell back against the headboard. Then she leaned forward and dropped her face into her hands. Her head was pounding in thick throbbing beats. Anxiety churned in her belly, and a too-familiar sense of helplessness threatened to drown her in despair. *Every time I think I've put that bastard behind me, there he is again.*

Raven rolled out of bed and headed downstairs. She needed to talk to Kara.

And warn Nate, though the last thing she wanted was another conversation with him tonight.

* * *

Apparently Kara had told the others there was a problem. All three of them were clustered around the kitchen's prep island when she walked in. Nate looked up and winced under her gaze. Monique and Kara followed his gaze to her face, then turned to glower at him as if their suspicions had been confirmed. He looked away, his chiseled cheekbones darkening.

"Ron said the shit has hit the fan, but he didn't go into details." Kara turned back to the bottles and mixers arrayed on the counter front of her. Back in the day, working in bars had been the way she and Raven had paid the rent. Now she started mixing a Long Island Iced Tea. "What's the newest catastrophe?"

"Ewan's trying to get me charged with felony magic."

"What?" Everybody -- including Nate -- stiffened in alarm.

Kara swore viciously. "Shit. What'd he do?"

"Called a producer at *L.A. Morning* and accused me of singing Gary into a rage so he'd attack Roger. Then I had my pet bodyguard murder him."

Kara spat a stream of obscenity that made even Nate the ex-Marine blink. She handed over the drink, and Raven downed a mouthful of fire. "You need to sue that creep, Raven. If he wasn't a federal judge's kid, he'd be doing time."

Monique leaned an elbow on the counter and swirled her drink, frowning. "This Ewan -- I know he's an abusive prick, but what's this about a judge?" The Bard had only joined the band a few months before, after a prior backup singer quit to go solo.

Raven sighed. "Ewan comes from a very prominent family. His dad's Samuel Bradley, a federal judge. Which means he's got a lot of pull. The Bradleys are a Bard clan, though Ewan's the only one of them in entertainment."

"Because Ewan's the only one who has anything approaching a singing voice," Kara explained. "That's why the family's always been in law or politics, where they can influence voters and juries -- assuming they don't get caught at it."

Monique muttered, "Sometimes I think the fucking humanists have a point."

"Especially where Ewan's concerned," Kara agreed. "He's an only child, and he's spoiled as hell. Nothing was too good for him."

"And nothing he ever did was good enough." Raven downed another swallow of her drink, then reluctantly put it aside. She did not need to be hung over tomorrow. "Assuming he wasn't lying to me -- which may be a big assumption -- his father beat him like a drum when he was a kid."

Nate snorted. "I have great difficulty feeling sympathy for the fuckwad."

"How *did* you end up with this prince among assholes?" Monique asked.

"He was looking for a female lead singer for his punk band, Asmodeus. That was in '84. He saw me sing at a bar and offered me a job on the spot. Even hired Kara to do the visual effects for our tours." Raven stared into her glass as it sat on the counter, turning it between her fingers. "I thought we'd hit the big time."

"He also had a ton of money and threw plenty of it around," Kara agreed. "Gotta admit, he paid damn well. Too bad his voice doesn't match his Talent. That *Rolling Stone* reporter nailed it."

Monique blinked. "I haven't read it. What'd he say?"

Nate, who had, said, "And I quote: 'He's got the looks of Jim Morrison, only without the ability to either sing or write his way out of a paper bag.' Raven wrote Asmodeus's only hit."

Raven groaned. "Don't even mention that damned article. I wouldn't be in this mess if that asshole hadn't set Ewan off with that Morrison line. Besides, voice or no voice, he has plenty of Talent. Otherwise I'd have left him the first time he sent me to the ER."

Monique frowned. "You want to talk felony -- using magical influence on people you're abusing can get you serious time."

"Yeah, but the vics have to be able to prove what you did." Kara poured a *PowerUp* and handed it to Raven. "For the headache you're getting," she said. As Raven murmured thanks, she turned back to Monique. "And when Daddy is a federal judge, getting *anybody* to investigate is basically impossible, even without the judge using Talent. And Ewan really is good. I had a front row seat on his bullshit, but at one point he had even *me* thinking he was a good guy. And I hated his fucking guts at the time."

"His problem is he doesn't quite have the juice to punch his Talent through a recording. People love him in person, but on an album or broadcast, he's kinda... eh. So he doesn't get the record sales," Raven explained. "He can influence record execs into giving him a contract, but when the sales don't materialize, they drop him. And now he's got a shitty track record *and* a rep for using his power on execs, so none of them will let his ass in the door."

Monique's frown had deepened. "So how did you manage to kick him to the curb?"

"I made a charm for her that could block Bard talent," Kara explained. "Gave her some resistance."

"That last night, he'd had a fight with his father - - who was threatening to cut him off again if he didn't quit the Merlin. Then he'd found out the label was doing a single of the song I'd sung lead on. So as usual, Ewan decided to take it all out on me. It was the worst beating he'd ever given me." Nate made a low growling sound, but she ignored him. "The whole time, he ranted that my constant fucking up was the real reason Asmodeus wasn't the success it should be. That I was sabotaging him, making him feel his voice wasn't good enough."

Kara took a deep slug of her drink. "Her real sin was warning him smoking Merlin was going to destroy his vocal cords."

"Then he *really* cut loose. I don't remember anything after that until I woke up in the ER." She grimaced, remembering the brutal headache from the concussion and the stabbing pain of her broken arm.

"I found her lying in the floor in a puddle of blood and called 911," Kara said. "While she was in surgery, I called the judge and told him that if he didn't put a leash on his son, I was going to go to the media with the pictures of her injuries and accuse Ewan of felony magic. I knew the judge couldn't allow that line of thought, because he'd been doing the same fucking thing to people for years. So he hauled on Ewan's choke chain and made him back down."

Raven took another deep swallow of her *PowerUp*. Her headache was beginning to fade. "I had years of blessed peace, until that damn *Rolling Stone* article a year and a half ago."

Kara nodded. "Worst thing you can do to a narcissist is make him look bad in national media." Her eyes narrowed. "Weird how just a week later, that reporter was mugged and badly beaten." She made air quotes with her fingers. "Just a 'random street crime.'"

Monique's eyes widened. "Ewan actually beat him up?"

Nate snorted. "Oh, hell no. That coward only beats women. But I'd be willing to bet he hired someone to do it."

"I mean," Raven drawled bitterly, "It's not like the law applies to the Bradleys."

Monique shook her head. "You've made some bad enemies, girlfriend."

Raven sighed and drained the last of her *PowerUp*. "Yeah, I have noticed that."

* * *

Nate headed down the hall to Raven's office, with its floor-to-ceiling bookshelves crammed with books, Grammys and MTV Moonmen serving as bookends. He picked up the phone sitting on the antique art deco desk and punched an outside line. He hated to wake Bruce up, but they both needed to be on hand for this.

His partner picked up on the fifth ring, sounding as wide-awake as if he was expecting an artillery barrage. "I knew I shouldn't have gone home. What shit hit the fan now?"

"Ewan's been at it again," Nate told him, and outlined the situation in a few clipped sentences.

"Shit," Bruce growled. "I'll have Mary drop me

off at the studio at seven so I can keep an eye on the motherfucker."

Nate hesitated, but Bruce deserved to know, so he added, "There's one more thing. Raven and I..." He broke off to search for the words to explain just how thoroughly he'd fucked up.

Before he could even finish the thought, his friend sighed. "I knew this was coming. Between the obvious sexual tension and today's episode of *Wild Kingdom*, it was inevitable."

"She says she's in love with me." Mentally, Nate cursed. He hadn't intended to say it.

"Hey, terrific!"

Nate scowled. "Not given the shelf life of all her other romances this year."

"You mean the social-climbing Primo and the actor whose career passed its sell-by date three years ago?" Bruce asked dryly. "Yeah, who wouldn't find happiness with *those* princes?"

"Both of them were a damn sight better looking than me," Nate said, feeling distinctly off-balance. He'd been sure his partner would chew him out over this.

"On the other hand, *you* just saved her life at considerable risk to your own."

"Exactly," Nate said. "This is gratitude and the aftermath of a near-death experience. Not exactly the foundation for lasting relationship."

"You know, I could've sworn you were smarter than this."

"Wow. Thanks."

"Have you *ever* paid attention to the way she looks at you? I spotted it even before she started dating the two weasels. In fact, I'd be willing to bet you're the *reason* she started dating the two weasels."

He blinked. "What do you mean by that?"

"Well, think about it. The last guy she thought she was in love with beat her on a regular basis. I'd be willing to bet she'd doesn't trust her own judgment when it comes to men. But *you* damn near died for her. You've proved you're not a sociopath."

"That's a fucking low bar." He sighed. "Women like Raven Garland don't fall in love with guys like me."

"Is that you talking, or your star-hating mama?"

For the second time in the conversation, Nate's jaw dropped. "My mom has nothing to do with this."

"Yeah, sure she doesn't. I'll see you tomorrow. In the meantime, try to grow a brain."

* * *

Nate squinted against the studio lights and used every ounce of discipline he'd learned as his father's son to keep his face expressionless.

He, Kara, Raven and her lawyer, Andrew Eagleton, sat on the raised dais in four uncomfortable lemon-yellow chairs so tall, he'd had to help the women up into the seats. Three hulking TV cameras glided silently around them, while studio lights attached to overhead grids blazed into their faces. He could feel sweat trickling down his spine as he began to bake in the dark gray suit he wore whenever he needed to look like Secret Service. He was acutely conscious of the tiny lavaliere microphone curled and clipped neatly to his red silk tie.

Raven looked cool and professional in a boxy crimson Christian Dior power suit that practically screamed, *"Fuck with me at your peril."* Kara wore flowing black slacks and a powder blue jacket that showed off a demure white silk blouse. Eagleton looked every inch the expensive lawyer, graying and handsome in a blue pinstripe suit and a toothy Crest commercial smile, eyes as black and flat as a great white's.

LA Morning's host Jonathan Storm, a broad-shouldered thirty-something Bard, wore a double-breasted black suit, his tie wine-red over a white shirt, his dark hair flawlessly styled to make the most of his GQ features. His eyes were cool and hard and avid as he fired questions at Raven based entirely on her stalker's lies.

Hiding his outrage took everything Nate had.

"Your ex-husband claims you used your abilities to make Gary Handle lose control of his cat and attack your director. Here's what he said earlier this morning..."

Nate's shoulders tensed as Ewan Bradley's face flashed on the TV monitor set into the wall. Out of the corner of one eye, he saw Raven stiffen, her face going expressionless.

The *Rolling Stone* reporter was right: Bradley did look like Jim Morrison. Same angular jaw, full mouth set in a permanent pout. His eyes were large and brown in a way that should have been soulful but wasn't. Probably because his expression was off, as if he were missing some crucial brain circuitry most humans had.

Apparently trying to emphasize the resemblance to the Doors frontman, he wore his dark hair in a messy mop of curls. However, Morrison had been only twenty-seven when he died, and Ewan was a decade older. What's more, despite skillful makeup, he looked hollow-eyed and so thin as to be gaunt.

The vivid emerald suit didn't help. It was probably intended to look rock-star flamboyant, but it only made him look sallow and unhealthy.

"Raven has always been ruthless when it comes to her power," Ewan said, his voice resonant. "If you make her mad, she won't hesitate to use her Talent to see you suffer. My sources on the crew tell me Timmons ignored her 'creative ideas.'" He made air quotes with long, bony fingers. "She *hates* that. Hates it when you don't appreciate her 'genius.' My friend on the crew told me she worked the Feral, made him madder and madder until he finally… snapped. The only reason the cops didn't charge her is because she used her Talent to influence them."

The image froze, and Storm lifted a brow. "What's your response to these accusations?"

Nate had to work harder than he ever had in his career to keep the sheer screaming rage off his face.

"This is ridiculous slander," Eagleton said, in a voice so rich and deep, it was a shame he wasn't a Bard. "My client has a restraining order against her ex-husband for his abusive treatment of her. This is just more of the same."

"Okay," Storm said dismissively, not looking away from his target. "Raven, what's your response to these accusations?"

"First off, Roger's a friend, and I'd never do anything to hurt him. Second, I don't use my Talent that way -- not on cops, and certainly not a Feral who could have killed *everyone* there. Including me," Raven said with frigid dignity, anger burning in her green eyes. "Finally, what he's talking about is felony magical murder. I'd have to be an idiot to risk the death penalty because I was in a snit."

"I was there," Nate said, unable to keep his mouth shut any longer. "Mr. Timmons didn't ignore any of her suggestions. In fact, he was about to incorporate one of them when Mr. Handle attacked him."

Storm turned that predatory stare on him. "So you're saying Mr. Bradley doesn't know what he's talking about?"

"No, I'm saying he's lying. Every word of that was a lie. Every. Single. Word. Ms. Garland doesn't misuse her Talent. And she has a *lot* of it. Handle practically tore Mr. Timmons' arm off, and he was in agony. She sang to numb his pain with so much power, not only did he stop screaming, everyone in the room got high. I've watched her play concerts for months, but even I had no idea just what she can do when she cuts loose. I had to ask her to stop so the ambulance crew could work."

"He's right," Kara agreed. "I'd also like to add that when it comes to misusing Talent, Ewan is the expert. I saw him do it to Raven every time he beat her. He always made her think it was her fault. She honestly believed that. As to as to influencing the cops to drop a case, he'd know all about that too. There's a reason he wasn't charged after he put her in the hospital the last time."

Storm's eyes widened and flicked to Raven's face. She didn't even flinch. "Is this true?"

"Yes," she said flatly. "We'd been married for two years, and he beat me a dozen times, several of them bad enough to send me to the ER. And every single time he used his Talent to convince me I was at fault. That's why I never filed a report until I ended up in the hospital the last time." She reached into her huge red shoulder bag and pulled out a manila folder. "I have the medical records and photos here."

She passed them to Storm, who started flipping through them with narrowed, calculating eyes.

"We were supposed to go out to lunch that day,"

Kara said. "When I arrived at their apartment, I found her lying unconscious in the kitchen floor. I called an ambulance. I have no idea where Ewan was, other than not at home. He'd just left her there in her own blood. I took pictures. You'll find them in the file."

Storm's eyebrows lifted, and he raised one of the prints. "Get a shot of this, Johnny."

Nate didn't look at the photo -- he already remembered it a little too well from the research he'd done when he and Bruce took the contract. Raven lay sprawled in the floor, out cold. Both eyes were swollen shut, blood smeared her chin from her split lip, and one forearm was black with bruising, the bones bent in the middle of the forearm in a compound break. Blood puddled around the back of her head, and a broken broom stick lay next to her body, snapped off above just above the broom head, which lay a few feet away.

"You took photos when your friend was lying unconscious?" Storm asked, incredulous.

Kara met his eyes defiantly. "Yeah, after I'd called the ambulance. I knew what he was capable of, and I knew damn well I'd better document what he'd done if I had any hope of getting her away from him. I had no doubt he'd use his Talent to keep the cops from charging him."

Storm was a Bard, and he knew the law as well as they did. "As Raven said, using Talent to influence police officials conducting an investigation is both felony magic *and* obstruction of justice." He looked down at the photo. To Nate's surprise, he looked slightly sick. Maybe Storm wasn't a complete shit after all. "Why did he *do* this?"

Kara scowled. "He's an abusive f... creep."

Raven gave her a look and Kara closed her mouth, though she looked mutinous.

Raven met the host's gaze, her expression more weary than angry now. "Our manager had just told him the label wanted to release the song I sang lead on as a single, rather than one of his."

"And being a sociopath..." Nate muttered.

"I was sweeping the kitchen when he stormed in," she continued. "Ewan yanked the broom away from me and snapped it in two. He whipped the stick across my chest so hard, he broke three ribs, then bashed me across the face. I thought he was going to kill me, so I tried to sing him into calming down and stopping. Big mistake. The minute I opened my mouth, he completely lost it. Picked me up off the floor and slammed me into the kitchen counter so hard, my arm snapped like that broom. My head hit the floor, and that's the last thing I remember."

"You're lucky you're not dead," Storm said, then winced as if suddenly wary of possible lawsuits. "Assuming that is what happened."

"It's what happened," Kara said. "While she was undergoing surgery on her arm, I called... ah, some people who knew him..." Nate knew she meant the judge. "I made it clear to them that Raven had been badly hurt, and they said they'd have a word with him."

Which is to say, the judge threatened had him with being disowned if he didn't leave her the hell alone. The elder Bradley had been well aware his son was one blown cover-up away from becoming a huge scandal.

"When I came to, I realized it was only a matter of time before he killed me," Raven said. "The minute I was mobile, I served him with divorce papers. Didn't even go back for my things."

"Whereupon you went solo and became a huge

star," Storm said. "While Ewan went on to being known as a one-hit wonder. Bet he loves that." His smile was a bit ugly. Nate suspected he was now firmly in their corner.

"Did you file a police report?" the reporter asked. "There have been certain... rumors about your marriage, but when we checked, his record was clean. He was certainly never charged with domestic violence as severe as this." He waved the stack of photos and medical records.

"I filed a police report," Raven said. "I don't know why he wasn't charged."

Storm lifted a brow. "Think it has anything to do with his father being a Federal judge?"

"I have no idea," she said without so much as a flicker of an eyelid.

"But it's been years since your divorce. Why would he come after you now?"

"A *Rolling Stone* reporter compared Ewan to Jim Morrison, except without the singing voice or writing ability. It set him off. He's been stalking me ever since, making threatening phone calls and sending death threats. He even broke in one night. I had to hire Nate and his partner as bodyguards."

"Judging by what happened yesterday, that was money well spent." Storm turned to Nate. "Do you consider her ex-husband a serious threat?"

"Yes, I do," Nate said. He handed the Bard a stack of photocopies of the death threats they'd received. "We got the one on the top just yesterday."

Storm frowned as he flipped through the gory images. "These look like crime scene photos with her face taped over the murder victim's. Where'd he get them?"

"I have no idea," Nate said flatly. "But yes, I

consider him a very serious threat. Raven is not going to end up like Rebecca Schaeffer on my watch." In 1989, the young sitcom star had been murdered by a man who'd stalked her for years. He'd been furious because she'd appeared in a love scene. The thought of Raven dying like that had haunted Nate for months.

"Do you believe Ewan's the one who drove Gary Handle to attack the director?" Storm asked him.

Nate blinked, since the thought had never occurred to him. "Actually, no. Handle was a respected Arcane Corps officer until his tiger was killed in a training exercise a few months ago, and he melded with it. Under normal circumstances Melds like Gary are perfectly stable, but that soon after they fuse, the cat is still fairly upset about being killed."

Storm snorted. "Can't imagine why."

"They're short-tempered and potentially violent until the human learns how to manage his cat's emotions. Mr. Handle didn't yet have that kind of control."

Raven took up the story. "We'd had a big dance number choreographed for the video, but Gary had trouble with the choreography. I think his cat was upset about being in such a stressful situation with so many strangers, and Gary couldn't concentrate. Anyway, we ended up scrapping the scene. He became increasingly angry."

"I could tell he was beginning to lose control," Nate said. Probably best not to admit he'd tried to get them to fire Gary. "I took Raven and Roger aside to warn them of what to do if he lost control. Unfortunately, I'd never had much chance to work with Ferals in the Marines. I didn't realize how keen their hearing is. He overheard me, and it set him off."

"Speaking of surprising abilities, our Feral

consultant said what you did -- punching through Gary's manifestation like that -- should have been impossible. How did you manage it?"

Nate shrugged. "I'm a Primo."

"A *dancer?*" Storm's brows quirked in surprise. "I thought you were a bodyguard."

"Dancing's not the only way you can focus magic. You can also do it through any physical movement. My father was a Marine drill instructor, and he taught me and my brothers martial arts from the time we could walk. We learned how to use our power to amplify our strength and speed. When I was a kid, I figured out how to focus all my magic into one fist." He smiled faintly. "Until yesterday, all I'd done with it was win a drunken bet by putting my fist through a car door."

Storm blinked. "Didn't that break every bone in your hand?"

He shrugged. "I learned how to shield it with my magic."

"How the hell does that work?"

Nate snorted. "Do I look like a quantum physicist to you?"

"I'm told you have a Bronze Star for defending your unit against an attack by one of Saddam Hussein's Ferals during Desert Storm. Did you punch him too?"

"No, I used my M-16 on full auto and blasted his manifestation until it collapsed and I could kill him. That won't work with a pistol, since you need high-velocity rounds." He shrugged. "I was desperate -- the tiger was going after Raven. I used my childhood trick - and it worked."

Storm grinned. "So you're a superhero?"

Nate winced, imagining how his father would

react to that. "No, I'm *lucky*. As I said, I was a kid when I came up with the idea. It just happened to work."

"You still took a big chance. He'd have killed you if it hadn't," Raven said.

Nate looked away, uncomfortable. "He'd have killed me regardless."

"Not if you'd run."

He snorted. "Not an option."

Storm looked from Nate's face to hers. The knowing look in the reporter's eyes made Nate wonder uneasily what his own had just shown.

Chapter Five

When they stepped offstage, Bruce was waiting for them, looking tall and professional in a dark blue suit and tie. "No sign of Ewan," he said, and rolled his shoulders. "We're going have to hire more people. My shoulder blades are itching."

"Yeah, so are mine," Nate said grimly. He'd forgotten how God-awful those photos were. What Ewan had done to her had sent his anger leaping dangerously high. And the fact that the bastard was now trying to scuttle her career only added to his fury.

He forced himself to breathe in and out slowly, fighting to regain control. Anger that hot could make you stupid.

A production assistant showed them to the rear exit the station used when someone needed to leave out the back, and they all started toward the limo.

"I guess that precious career of yours is *toast* now," a nasty voice mocked. "Told you you'd regret what you did to me, bitch." Ewan laughed, the sound snide.

Nate whirled as the stalker spun and darted away. "Get them out of here!" he snapped at Bruce and shot down the alley after him.

It was past time the bastard found out what it felt like to be on the receiving end of a beating.

* * *

"Go after them!" Raven yelled at Bruce. "Nate needs backup!"

"No." The big man braced a hand on her and Kara's shoulders and urged them toward the car. "My responsibility is to get you to safety. Nate can handle that asshole."

"But anything could happen! What if Ewan's got a gun? What if..." Raven could tell from the stony look on his face that Bruce wasn't going to listen.

Unless she *made* him. It was wrong, and she knew it, but she didn't give a shit. All she could think about was Nate up against Ewan. Alone.

Nate was bigger and stronger, but against a Bard with as much power as Ewan, that didn't mean much. Ewan might not be the greatest singer, but he could make you believe the sky was green plaid when he wanted to.

Or that you deserved the broken ribs he'd just given you with a kick in the side.

Raven met Bruce's eyes. "*Go after them!*" she snarled, pumping power into her voice. "Nate needs you. *And if you don't get to him, he could die!*"

Bruce's eyes widened and went unfocused. Without another word, he sprinted in the direction the other two had gone.

Kara stared after him, her jaw dropping. "*Raven!* He's going to quit! You just violated his contract!"

"He can sue the shit out of me as long as he helps Nate," Raven said flatly. "Get in the car. We're going after them." Whether they'd be able to track them in rush hour traffic was another question.

* * *

The little bastard was fast, Nate would give him that, his gaze focused on Ewan's fleeing back. The Bard had changed out of the emerald suit, and now he was dressed in black jeans and a tee, along with black Air Jordans a lot more suited to running than Nate's hard dress shoes. And to make matters worse, the crowd milling along the sidewalk made it damn near impossible to gain on him. Nate bellowed at people to get the hell out of the way, shoving men inside, ducking around women, old people and kids, ignoring outraged shouts and middle fingers.

All his attention was focused on Ewan's narrow back. He was tempted to draw his gun, but shooting the prick would be murder. Assuming, that is, he didn't hit some other poor bastard who got in the way. Especially since it didn't appear the Bard was armed.

Through the crowd ahead, he saw Ewan duck into an alley, and Nate ducked and dodged after him, afraid he'd lose the little shit.

But when he rounded the corner, he spotted Ewan just as he turned down a side street. Seemed the bastard's Merlin addiction hadn't been great for his wind -- he was slowing down. The crowd was thinner here, and Nate was gaining.

Ewan veered down another alley. Nate lengthened his stride, pouring magic into his muscles now. He shot around the corner to see Ewan standing in front of a brick wall, panting and desperate. *Ha! Dead end! Outsmarted yourself this time, you fucker!*

The Bard turned, hands lifted as he panted, "Don't be too... too... hasty here. Let's... Let's talk..."

Nate took one long stride forward, pulling back his fist. "We can talk *after* I give you a little taste of your own medi..."

Magic blasted from the ground, flashed up the length of his body, and locked every muscle he had. He tripped over his own feet and went down hard, the impact clipping his teeth together on his tongue. He tasted blood.

Shit! Shit shit shit! Nate, you dumb bastard... Fighting to breathe, he squeezed his eyes shut.

Oh. Hell! He was surrounded by a ring of glowing shapes that rotated slowly through the air just above his head. Sigils. *It's an Arcanist booby trap! Fuck!*

But that was impossible. Bards couldn't do that kind of magic...

"You fucked... up now, you... you arrogant asshole," Ewan wheezed.

Nate pried his eyes open to focus on the man, who was bent over, hands braced on his knees, smirking even as he fought to breathe. Damn, he was out of shape. Nate was irritated he'd let the bastard outrun him even this long.

"You just *had*... to touch what's mine... motherfucker. Everything that happens... Happens from here on out... is your own... fucking fault. Trying to play... play *hero*." His mouth twisted in a terrifying grin. "Well, you're gonna be... be her destruction instead. Raven'll give herself... Give herself up to get... you back... and I'm gonna kill *both* of you."

He straightened and signaled.

A woman stepped out from behind the dumpster at the rear of the alley. Red-haired, pale, and almost painfully thin in ripped stonewashed jeans and a crop top, she looked at most twenty-five. Her facial features were thoroughly ordinary, but when Nate dropped his lids, she blazed with power.

And there's the Arcanist that laid this Goddamn trap.

The woman crouched on the other side of the circle. Her blue eyes met his, too wide, the pupils blown. *Stoned as hell*, Nate thought.

Grinning, she touched a finger to the pavement, and he felt a wave of magic roll over him. Pain hit him between the eyes, so agonizing he couldn't bite back the scream.

* * *

Bruce ran, his dress shoes slapping the concrete as he fought desperately to make up for lost time. He could feel the sweat rolling off his body inside his suit, but he ignored it. The only thing that mattered was getting to Nate before Ewan killed him.

In the back of his mind, he knew he was violating procedure in leaving Raven alone. What was to stop Ewan from doubling back and snatching her? *I should turn around, get her ou...*

No, Nate's more important. Raven said so, and she's right.

But where in hell did they go? He'd lost them, and Nate was going to die. And...

He heard a scream from up ahead. Nate's voice, roaring pain and fury. Bruce stretched out and ran with every ounce of speed he had.

Another anguished bellow sent him darting down a side street. He slowed down, scanning, and heard something coming from an alley to his left. He spun toward it...

And saw a redheaded woman standing in the open door of a black panel van, a sprawled dark form lying at her feet.

"Nate!" Bruce shouted.

The woman looked up and smirked as she slammed the door closed.

Who the fuck is that?

The van fishtailed in a circle and roared toward him. Bruce barely threw himself aside in time to avoid getting hit. As it flew past, he saw Ewan in the driver's seat, face stretched in a manic grin.

Bruce raced after the van, desperately trying to get a look at its license tag. But it was moving too fast, accelerating away as it caught a lucky break in the traffic. He was able to make out only the letters RG, and even those he wasn't sure of.

He swore, and turned to see a familiar limo screech to a halt, Raven leaning to unlock the passenger door. Bruce hopped inside. "Go!" he roared. "They loaded him into a black van headed that way. I don't know if we can catch it, but..."

"We'll damn well give it our best shot!" Raven accelerated, ignoring the furious horns that blew behind them.

But there was no sign of the van as he told them what happened.

"He was unconscious?" Raven demanded. "Or dead?" There was raw terror in her voice, and her face was white as she threw him a desperate look, green eyes pools of anxiety.

"If he was dead, they'd have left him there. Hauling a body around L.A. is risky." Bruce's whole body vibrated with the need to chase Ewan, save Nate, even as his battle-honed experience insisted they were in the wind.

And now that Bruce thought about it, his own panic seemed out of proportion. He'd fought in combat, led men, even *lost* men, and he usually held it together better than...

His gaze fell on Raven's bone-white profile and desperate snarl. Realization hit. "You did something to me," he growled, anger blasting through the compulsion she'd laid on him. Suddenly he could think again. "Where the fuck do you get off? I could Goddamn have you charged!"

He saw he was right when she winced. "He was going to die, Bruce! I couldn't save him, and now Ewan's got him, and..."

At that reminder, he deflated, staring at her.

From the backseat, Kara said quietly, "She's in love with him, Bruce. What would Mary have done?"

Bruce cursed. His wife would have done the exact same thing if she'd had the power and he'd been in danger. "Fine," he snapped, and pointed a forefinger at Raven. "But if you ever, *ever* use your Talent to compel me to do anything again, that's *it*. It's a violation of our contract, and I will sue the fuck out of you."

She shot him an apologetic glance. "Yeah, I won't do that again." Then, her voice hardened. "Unless it's Nate's life. Then..."

Well, at least she fucking cares about him as more than muscle.

As she drove furiously, weaving through traffic and hissing curses, he looked over his shoulder at Kara and Monique in the backseat. "One of you call the cops. I was able to get a couple of letters of the tag number. The LAPD can at least..."

"We can't afford to do that," Raven interrupted. "He's got a habit of buying off people high in the police department. I'm quite sure he did it this time too."

"So offer a bigger bribe!" Bruce snapped. "You've got more money than that asshole."

Raven snorted. "But my daddy's not a judge."

"Where is this alley?" Kara asked suddenly. "That woman you're talking about... I'm wondering if she's the reason they were able to knock Nate out. I can't see that asshole Ewan being able to do it. Nate would eat him alive."

The light dawned, and Bruce's eyes widened. "You think that woman is an Arc? That she laid a booby trap?" God knows he'd encountered plenty of those in the 'Storm. Saddam Hussein's fucking Arcanists were the only reason the US and its allies hadn't been able to roll over the Iraqis like a tank over a Lego set.

He started giving directions back to the scene of

Nate's kidnapping.

Minutes later they pulled into the alley, and Raven stopped the car.

All three women closed their eyes and stared through the windshield. "Shit!" It was a chorus.

"Yeah, that's a spell," Kara said grimly.

Bruce scanned the area, but he couldn't see anything. No surprise. As a Norm, he couldn't perceive magic unless a spell used enough power to bleed into the visible spectrum.

"I need a closer look," Kara said, and they all piled out of the car.

She walked over to the center of the alley and stopped, staring down at the ground. "*That* is one big-ass magic circle." She crouched, examining the pavement more closely. "She used infrared paint to draw it. If Nate was running full out, he wouldn't have been able to close his eyes. He must have run right into it."

Bruce frowned. "How could she be sure he wouldn't circle around it?"

She stood. "It's the width of the entire alley. The minute he turned the corner, it hit him like a brick to the face."

* * *

Raven stared at the ghostly magical shapes -- glowing on the ground against the darkness of her eyelids. She knew a few sigils, but she didn't recognize any of these. Reading magical symbols was a lot like reading music, though there were a hell of a lot more sigils than musical notations.

Her stomach clamped into a ball of sick nausea. "Where did they take him?" She barely recognized her own high, ragged voice. "Is he even still alive?"

"Maybe the judge knows something," Kara

suggested. "If he even knows what property Ewan owns, that would give us a place to look."

"Worth a try." They got back into the car, though with Bruce behind the wheel this time. As he started the car, Raven picked up the car phone and hit the number she'd programmed for Judge Bradley's piranha of a lawyer.

She had to spend fifteen interminable minutes working her way through assistants before Ari Greenfield picked up. "Miss Garland," he began his voice laced with cold anger. "My client does not appreciate your dragging his name through the media."

"If he thinks that interview was bad, wait until Ewan murders my bodyguard. Whom he just kidnapped using an Arcanist booby trap. Which, by the way, is definitely felony magic. I need to know where the bastard took my bodyguard, *and* I need the judge to make it damn clear to the police department that they'd better not drag their feet looking for him! Otherwise, this scandal will be so epic, Sam will wish he'd never fathered that little sociopath."

"He already does," the lawyer snapped back. "Look, my client retired last week. He has no authority to tell the police anything. In any case, he's disowned Ewan, and hasn't spoken to him in years. He would have no idea where he is or what he intends to do. Ewan is a grown man, and it's time he faced the consequences of his actions."

"And it's time the judge faced the consequences of his shitty parenting," Raven snapped back. "Call him wherever he is, on the Riviera or wherever. Tell him to *call me* or I will sing like a bird to *60 fucking Minutes.*" Raven slammed down the phone. Then she sat forward and buried her face in her hands.

The phone rang and Raven pounced on it without checking caller ID. "If you have any idea at all..." she began.

"Hello, Raven," Ewan said, his voice gloating. "I've been looking forward to this for a very long time."

Ice rolled up the length of her body from her heels to her hairline. Everyone in the car froze, their gazes snapping to her face. "Give Nate back." Command rang in her voice, her magic lashing out with power enough to reach even through the phone's mechanics.

"Oh, very fierce. But no, it's not going to be that easy."

"What exactly do you want?" Her heart pounded in her ears.

"You. Or your boyfriend is going to find himself powering a very nasty spell. Go home and wait until I call. And don't even *think* about calling the police, because I'll know. I still have my contacts on the force, and they're even more highly placed now than they were years ago." The phone clicked and a buzz sounded in her ear. The handset tumbled from nerveless fingers. Kara caught it and hung it up in the cradle.

"No," Bruce said coldly. "That fucker is just playing with you. He'll kill you *and* Nate, and Nate wouldn't want that. I'll get on the phone and call some guys I know -- other bodyguards. We'll get him back."

"They're more likely to shoot him *for* Ewan," Raven told him. "The bastard's Talent may not carry well over of a recording, but it's more than good enough in person. God knows he could always make me jump through hoops."

"Which is exactly why you shouldn't go

anywhere near him. All that will accomplish is you joining Nate in whatever circle they've got him in."

"Not if we appear to give Ewan what he wants." Raven met his gaze in the rearview mirror. "I can distract him, get him focused on me."

"And I have some charms to protect us from his voice," Kara said. "I just need to freshen the charge on them, and we'll be set."

Bruce glowered at her in the rearview. "*Us?* Oh, I don't think so."

"When was the last time you disarmed an Arcanist booby trap, Bruce?"

Bruce, mouth open for his next salvo, stopped in mid-rant. He cursed savagely. "I still need to call my guys..."

"There isn't going to be time," Raven said. "Ewan is a psychotic asshole, but he's not stupid. He may be watching. You and Kara are going to have to follow me in another car."

"And me," Monique put in calmly. "You and me singing together may be able to get the fucker under control." She wrapped her long, dark fingers around Raven's. They felt warm against her icy flesh.

"You don't have to do that," Raven managed, touched at her friends' loyalty.

Monique gave her a flash of white teeth. "Nate risked his life to save us yesterday. What kind of asshole would I have to be to stay at home? Besides, I'm a damn good shot. My daddy took me hunting when I was a kid."

Raven turned her hand and squeezed Monique's. "I don't like this, but... You're right. You do have a hell of a lot of power, and we could use you. Thank you."

"Yeah, well, you're both nuts," Bruce growled. "And Nate's going to be pissed."

"I just want Nate to be alive to *be* pissed," Raven told him. "And this is the best way to make sure of it."

* * *

Raven watched anxiously as Kara sketched a magic circle on the floor and knelt in the center of it, then arranged four small clay charms in front of her knees.

Because they worked in a business full of unscrupulous magic users, her Arc friend kept a supply of charms designed to shield against magical influences. All she had to do now was make sure they were properly charged.

The house phone rang even as her power rose.

Raven pounced on the phone. "I want to talk to Nate before I'm going anywhere," she snapped, trying to buy time. "For all I know, you've already killed him."

"All right." There was laughter in Ewan's voice, an ugly note she knew entirely too well. She heard his boots click on the floor as he paced restlessly, accompanied by a familiar creak. He was probably wearing those damn leather pants he put on whatever he was trying to channel Morrison. "Talk to your girlfriend," he said.

There was only silence. Raven flicked her eyes to Kara, who made a stretching gesture with both hands. She needed to buy little more time.

At the kitchen table, Bruce was loading guns, his mouth set in grim lines. Monique helped him, her hands flying.

"I said *talk to your girlfriend,*" Ewan snarled, and even over the phone, Raven felt the punch of his power.

"Stay the fuck away!" Nate hissed into the phone through his teeth. "The bastard's going to just kill both of us. I'm in a..." His voice cut off in a grunt that sounded like suppressed pain.

"He is a stubborn bastard," Ewan said, his voice casual. "I actually think the fucker believes he loves you. You really have scrambled his brains, haven't you?"

"If you hurt him, I'm going to scramble yours!" Raven snarled, trembling with rage.

"You won't do jack shit. I don't care how many million records you sold, you're *nothing*. You've always been nothing and you'll always be nothing."

The words came out of her mouth without stopping at her brain. "I'm a hell of a lot more than you have ever been," Raven spat. "And that's the whole problem, isn't it? All that money couldn't buy you the one thing you wanted: a voice. You couldn't sing lead in a high school musical."

The minute the words were out of her mouth she mentally cursed herself.

"Bitch, you're gonna pay for that."

Nate cried out in pain, and her heart lurched.

"Be at the corner of Bard and Arcane Avenue in fifteen minutes or he's dead. Come alone." The phone buzzed.

* * *

Fifteen minutes later, Raven was staring at a pay phone on the corner of Bard and Arcane.

She'd taken the limo while Bruce followed, hanging well back in his own nondescript sedan. She pulled over and stalked toward the pay phone just as it began to ring. She jerked up the handset and growled, "I saw this movie. Originality has never been your strength, has it?"

"Gable and Sorcerer Street," Ewan replied, and hung up.

Raven ran back to her car, threw herself behind the wheel, and gunned it toward the next stop.

* * *

The rat writhed and fought, hissing in terror. Ewan's pet Arcanist had bound it to the floor on its back with pieces of duct tape stretched over its furry belly. Its claws scrabbled uselessly at the air as its jaws snapped.

Nate had never cared for rats, but this one was pure white with pink eyes. They must have bought it at a pet store, along with the other twelve rats arranged just inside the magic circle.

The others were all dead. Their blood filled the inch-deep indentation the bastards had carved into the stage floor. *The owner of this joint is really going to regret renting to these loons.*

Nate had awakened half an hour ago in the circle's center, his torso, arms, and legs taped down with layer after layer of duct tape. He could have freed himself easily enough -- he had, after all, punched through that damned tiger.

The problem was that the tape was just reinforcement. The real binding was the immobilization spell the bitch had laid on him before he even regained consciousness. It lay over him like a lead cloak, suppressing his Primo magic.

The redhead Arc -- Ewan called her Crystal -- paced just beyond the ring of furry corpses, smoking a hand-rolled cigarette. Judging by the acrid reek and the way her hand shook, it was uncut Merlin.

She held a butcher knife in the other hand, the point dripping blood as she strode back and forth, a steady *plop plop plop*.

"The power of life and death," she said, her voice dreamy. "Man, you can't imagine how it feels. Power just pours into you, and it's like… being God." She sighed. "It's better than sex. It's better than Merlin. It's better than anything…"

Oh, great. She's babbling again. He tried to ignore the Arc in favor of focusing on the slow, rolling flex of his muscles.

It was a good thing these bastards had no idea how a Primo's power worked. They assumed her spell would prevent him from accessing his Talent, especially with the tape pinning him.

Fortunately, the spell didn't block his magic as completely as Crystal thought. He could still draw on it, though it wasn't easy. As for the tape, it was certainly a lot easier to work Primo magic when you could move freely. What they didn't realize was he could also build power by contracting each muscle group in turn. The rhythmic pulses of effort and intention would generate a magical charge he could use to weaken the immobilization spell.

Eventually.

"… And that's just from killing a rat. I can't wait to do you and your little bitch. Both of you together…"

Pacing faster, she took another deep drag of the cigarette, then wiped her running nose with the back of her hand. "When I was thirteen, I had this pet hamster. I'd read about sacrificial magic in this old, old spell book of my mom's. I drew a spell circle like the book said and knelt in the middle. Grabbed Mr. Wiggle's furry body in my hands and *squeezed* until I felt his little bones crunch. The power just… *rolled* over me. And it was the best thing *ever*."

Of all the kidnappers on the planet, I get Hanna Lecter, Nate thought, still flexing slowly. *Next she'll be pouring herself a nice Chianti.*

She took another drag and blew out a long

plume of smoke. "I told my mom Wiggles had gotten out of his cage and run away. Then I killed her teacup poodle. That was even better." *Draaaaaag.* "I killed for years and years. Cats. Dogs." She giggled, then went into a racking coughing fit. "I was total *hell* on the neighbors' pets. Mom knew. She knew what I was doing after the poodle, but she didn't tell dare tell anyone. She didn't want anybody to know. She wasn't supposed to have that book, much less let me get hold of it. She was afraid to even get me in therapy because she knew that a therapist would have a duty to report."

Crystal blew a plume of smoke at the lighting grid, flicking ashes on the floor to land in the blood trail from her knife. *Plop plop plop.* "Just kicked me out when I was sixteen. I think she knew I wanted to do *her* next." Her voice sounded dreamy. "I had a lot of power by then, so I started doing special effects for bands. That's how I met Ewan. I wanted to take the next magical step, but then they put that Arcanist to death for human sacrifice, and I didn't want to end up like *that.* I was very, very careful after that. And they never caught me. Because I'm *smart.*"

Keep smoking that shit, and you'll end up about as bright as a burned-out forty-watt.

Crystal stopped pacing and looked at him. "Time to finish the last sacrifice for the spell." Dropping to her knees, she lifted the knife. The rat hissed at her.

"Yeah, fuck you too," she told it, and stabbed straight down through the duct tape to bury the point in the floor with a *thunk.* The rat made a high-pitched squeal of agony.

Nate carefully did not close his eyes. He didn't want to watch her aura drink down the rat's life force.

Her eyes rolled back. She cried out, sounding

way too much like a woman having an orgasm.

When her shuddering stopped, Crystal opened her eyes to stare across the circle at him, her bloodshot eyes glittering in her thin, pale face, blown pupils surrounded by thin rings of ice-blue iris.

Nate flexed his muscles, fighting the hold of the tape. *I've got to get out of here. I'm not going to die like that fucking rat.*

"I was so alone until Ewan. Ewan understands me. Ewan knows about power. And he's great in the sack too." Her mouth spread in a grin Nate suspected he'd be seeing in his nightmares for years.

Assuming I live through this. His chances didn't look good.

Crystal rose and stepped over the rat's corpse, dripping knife in hand. Nate tensed, gathering what magic he'd managed to raise. She knelt and studied him with those wide, wide eyes. "You're pretty," she crooned. "Not as pretty as Ewan, but pretty." Lifting the knife, she pressed the tip to his cheekbone. "It's almost a shame."

Nate rammed power into his muscles, tried to surge free…

And the spell crashed down on him like a falling boulder, crushing him against the floor as if he suddenly weighed four hundred pounds. *Fuck.*

Crystal didn't even flinch at the thwarted rage on his face. It was possible she hadn't even noticed the attempt, as high as she was. "It's almost a shame." She gave him a bright smile, eyes glittering and crazed. "Maybe Ewan'll let me fuck you first. Maybe I can make that part of the ritual. They say there's a lot of power in sex."

I'd sooner screw one of the dead rats. It was probably as well they'd gagged him, or he'd have told her so.

"Crystal!" Ewan yelled from the kitchen. "Have you finished that fucking circle yet?"

"Yeah, it's done." She hopped up and hurried off.

Nate closed his eyes and watched the sigils orbiting faster around the circle. They were even brighter now, fed by the thirteenth rat's death.

He returned his attention to flexing his muscles, trying once again to build his magic. Praying he could do it in time.

Because the woman he loved was well on her way to getting herself killed.

"You sure she won't bring in the cops?" Crystal asked, walking back into the room at Ewan's side. "Or more bodyguards? Because she's a rock star. She's got enough money to hire an army."

"That bitch?" The Bard laughed, a plume of Merlin-scented smoke circling his head from the cigarette he held. The chuckle dissolved into a hacking cough. "She doesn't have the guts. I've got her thoroughly cowed. She won't dare risk his life." He hopped up on the stage and strolled over to grin viciously down at Nate. "Raven always was an idiot." He stepped over the ring of furry bodies to kneel beside Nate. "I'm actually doing you a favor. You'd have quickly found out that the pussy really wasn't worth dealing with her stupidity and ego." But the deep glitter of rage and jealousy in his eyes said something entirely different. "She's so damn stupid, she'll walk right into the circle and be astonished when we cut her throat." Ewan leaned closer. "And you'll have to watch. But that's what happens when you touch what's mine. And she was always mine. She's going to find that out today. And then I'm going to take everything I want. *Everything.*"

* * *

Raven stared out the windshield at the final address Ewan had given her. It was a redbrick building, considerably more run down than it had been the first time she'd seen it a decade ago. "You've got to be fucking kidding me."

Temper steaming, she parallel parked at the curb, then got out. She stared up at the sign jutting over the grimy sidewalk.

Red neon formed a cap with a red feather protruding at a jaunty angle. Just above that, yellow neon curled in intricate medieval-style lettering reading Will Scarlet's Tankard. The bar was named for Robin Hood's Bard companion, the troubadour who'd sung of the bandit archer's adventures with his Merry Men. Since it was early morning on a Monday, the bar was closed.

She'd met Ewan at Will Scarlet's. She'd been just seventeen, fronting the band she and Kara had formed in high school. Her mother was dead, and she'd been rooming with her friend, who worked as a bartender at Will's.

Ewan had listened to her sing a single set, then searched her out when the band had taken a break and offered her a job.

As much as she hated to admit it, it had been her big break. Ewan's money and social connections had given her a leg up on her career. But she'd paid for that chance. Holy God, how she'd paid.

Raven's mouth tightened as she started toward the front door, conscious of Bruce and the girls watching from Bruce's Honda, parked a block or so down the street. She didn't even glance toward them as she grabbed the door handle and pulled. She wasn't surprised to find it opened with the merry jingle of bells.

Fear skittered up her spine on clawed, icy feet as she walked in.

Chapter Six

"Ewan's being cute," Kara growled.

Monique glanced at her. "What?"

The Arcanist stabbed a finger at the neon sign. "That's the fucking bar where we met the creep. And it's also where she did the interview with that damned *Rolling Stone* reporter."

"Huh." Monique's brows lifted. "Bet he thinks he's clever."

As they watched, Raven opened the bar's door and walked in. No hesitation. No looking back.

"We've got to get in there before the fuckers kill her *and* Nate." Bruce cast a wary glance toward the front of the bar. It had two big picture windows, but he'd been careful to stop well short of them. "I parked in the bar's blind spot, but we still can't use the front door."

Kara pointed off across the street to their right. "That alley between the bar and the pizza joint next door? That's where they park the trucks for deliveries, and there's a kitchen entrance. Raven and I used it all the time."

Bruce grunted. "That'll work." They all got out and eased the car doors closed as quietly as they could before ducking between the buildings. "Keep an eye on the street," he murmured to Monique. "If you spot anybody coming, yell."

The Bard nodded and turned to watch the alley entrance, leaning a shoulder against one brick wall.

But when Bruce started into the alley, Kara held up a hand. "Let me check for booby traps." She closed her eyes a moment, then blew out a breath in relief. "If they have one, it's not out here."

Bruce tried the door, but the battered metal knob

didn't turn. Good thing he'd come prepared. Pulling out the set of lock picks he'd brought, he took a knee, glad he'd changed out of his suit. Jeans, a tee, and running shoes were definitely better suited to B&E. "Block the view, would you?" he murmured to Kara. "This isn't a particularly good neighborhood, but we don't want anyone calling the cops. With our luck, Raven's right and they'd warn these assholes."

Kara's brows lifted as he leaned in and inserted the picks. "You do that like you had a misspent youth."

He snorted. "I had an *Uncle Sam* youth. Sometimes he needs you to break into places and steal Iraqi shit." He leaned in to probe with his picks, feeling for the teeth of the locking mechanism. He was acutely conscious of every dragging second, of the way the woman leaning against the wall beside him shifted from foot to foot. Sweat broke out along his spine.

The tumblers finally yielded to his probing. Bruce turned the knob, then tucked away his picks. Drawing his weapon, he carefully pulled open the door, revealing the kitchen beyond. The equipment was as far from the spotless glory of Raven's kitchen as it was possible to get, but at least everything appeared relatively clean, if worn. The white stove had spots where the enamel had chipped away, and there was a dent in the oven door that was about the size of someone's head. The olive green vinyl flooring peeled up in places, marred by cigarette burns and stains.

He nodded at Kara, who leaned closer and closed her eyes as Monique joined them. After a moment, the Arcanist whispered, "I don't see any traps." She nodded to an open passageway at the other end of the room. "The bar is down that hall."

But as they started toward the barroom, a voice

stopped them on their tracks.

"I'm not doing shit until you let Nate go!" Raven snarled, and he felt the magical punch of her voice even through Kara's charm, hung on a cord around his neck.

"I said *get over here!*" Ewan snapped. His voice dropped to a deadly growl. "Or I'll come out and get you. And you don't want that."

* * *

Raven stared across the width of the room. Nate lay spread-eagle in the center of a magic circle, arms and legs immobilized under layer after layer of duct tape. His jacket, shoes and tie were gone, leaving him only in his slacks and white dress shirt. Drops of something red splattered the white fabric.

Blood? Has the bitch cut him? Fear and anger steamed through her.

But no. His gaze met hers, steady, though fury burned in his ice-gray eyes. Sigils rotated through the air around him and his two captors, glowing in shades of brilliant neon crimson. Raven frowned. She'd seen a hell of a lot of circles over the years, and judging by the glow of the magic, that one was incredibly powerful.

Could have something to do with the odd, humped shapes arranged around the circle, following its blinding crimson curve. She frowned, trying to figure out what they were...

Shit. Rats. Dead *rats.*

Thirteen furry corpses arranged nose to tail tip around the perimeter of the circle. Judging by the glossy coats - some white, some spotted - they were pets. No wonder the circle glowed with such intensity. The Arc had sacrificed animals to power it.

How much brighter will it blaze once they've killed me? "So, which is it going to be, lethal injection or the gas chamber?" Raven demanded with a lot more confidence than she felt. "Human sacrifice is an automatic death penalty in California."

To her satisfaction, she saw unease flicker across the face of the redheaded Arcanist at Ewan's side.

Ewan only laughed. "Like I told you before, I'm not at all worried." For once there was no punch of power to his voice, no effort to make her believe some lie.

"You're that confident you won't get caught?" How much time did she need to buy for the cavalry to arrive? Bruce had warned her that breaking in would probably take several minutes.

"How much Merlin *have* you smoked?" Raven sneered in a way she'd never have dared when they'd been married. But then, she wasn't that terrorized little girl anymore. "You look pretty stoned to me. I keep telling you, that shit's gonna be the death of you."

"Yeah, you always did say that, didn't you? And for once in your miserable life, you were right." The humor drained from his face, revealing churning rage just beneath it. Yet for once, it didn't seem to be directed at her. "I have lung cancer. Fourth stage -- it's spread pretty much everywhere. I'm dying." He laughed, the sound a bark of bitterness. "So you can see why I'm not worried about the state of California. If this doesn't work, I'll be dead long before they got the chance to kill me." Ewan bared his teeth. "So get your skinny little ass over here or we'll kill your boy toy right now."

Shit shit shit! She threw a quick look at the redhead, who shifted from foot to foot in excitement, anxiety forgotten. "How about you? Have *you* got cancer? Because they'll definitely put your ass to death."

"I'm perfectly healthy," the girl snapped. "And Ewan's going to be perfectly healthy too, once I use the magic I get from killing your whoring ass. Got me a healing spell allllllll ready to go."

Suddenly this whole thing made a lot of sense. "So it's not the *Rolling Stone* article you're pissed about. You'd be doing this anyway."

Ewan smirked. "Let's just say it made choosing the human sacrifice a lot easier."

Now that she looked at him, Raven could see how sick he was. She'd thought he'd looked haggard in the video she'd seen at the TV station, but she'd assumed it was just the Merlin. "It isn't going to work," she told the Arcanist. "He's, what?" She did a quick calculation. "Thirty-seven. The only way you'd be able to heal fourth stage lung cancer is if he was fourteen, and even then, it would be iffy. The bodies of adults don't respond to healing magic. Everybody knows that."

"But nobody's tried it with a human sacrifice powering the spell." The Arc's eyes glittered. "Not that you'll see it, because you'll be dead. Or else your gigolo will be."

The redhead stared at her, her expression fixed and feral. Raven had seen that look on Ewan's face enough time to recognize it. The bitch was higher than Alan Shepard's golf ball. They both were. Merlin was ramping up their magical abilities, but it was also increasing their paranoia and aggression. *If I step into that circle, I'll never walk out of it. But if I don't…*

Her eyes flicked to the butcher knife in the woman's hands. Its blade looked dark, crusted with drying blood…

Bruce, hurry the fuck up!

Which was when she heard the faintest scrape of

shoe leather against the floor coming from behind her. Her shoulders almost sagged in relief. *They're here!* She fought the impulse to look back over her shoulder. Instead she focused on the Arcanist as the woman moved over beside Nate's bound body and knelt. She raised the knife over his chest.

"Last chance, bitch," Ewan said. "Get in here, or we'll start without you."

The redhead's eyes fastened on Nate's face, and the grin on her face was chilling. Hungry. And not even remotely sane.

I've pushed this as far as I dare. "All right, all right!" Raven raised both hands and started toward the circle. "Just let Nate go!"

But they wouldn't. Ewan had always been a lying bastard who'd never kept a single one of his many, many promises. Especially when he promised not to hurt her. He *loved* hurting her. She'd sworn she'd never let him victimize her again, yet here she was. *This is insane.*

Raven met his cruel black gaze, and her stomach clenched with the need to run. But she couldn't. The bastards would kill Nate, and she wouldn't have let that happen even if she hadn't been blind in love with him.

"Damn, you were right about her." The redhead rose and stepped toward her circle, making a complicated gesture. The rotating sigils dimmed and sank as she lowered the shield to let Raven step inside…

A gun boomed, followed by two more firing -- a furious *crack crack crack* as Bruce, Kara and Monique began to fire. Raven dove for the floor on sheer instinct as ricochets whined like enraged wasps.

"Hold your fire!" Bruce barked over Monique

and Kara's shocked yelps.

Ewan and his Arcanist just stood there. Grinning.

As Raven looked over her shoulder, Bruce smacked his fist into empty air and swore in a stream of rage and creative obscenity. Kara and Monique stared at her in helpless horror.

"You were right," the Arc told Ewan.

"Of course I was right," he said with an ugly sneer in Raven's direction. "She cheated. She always cheats."

Raven closed her eyes. Bruce, Kara, and Monique were trapped on the wrong side of a glowing barrier of rotating sigils. Kara must have been distracted by Ewan's ranting and missed seeing it.

The fucking Arc had constructed a second circle enclosing the barroom, just feet beyond the kitchen entrance. The redhead had let Raven inside, then triggered it when her friends tried to enter.

Ewan smirked at her, smug and nasty. "Let's stop fucking around, Crystal. Let's kill this bitch."

* * *

Nate glared at Raven over his gag, silently ordering her to run. Fight. *Do something, for fuck's sake!*

Instead she planted herself just beyond the circle and glared defiantly at Ewan as he sauntered toward her, all arrogance. In five minutes, she was going to be in the circle, and she'd be lying beside him like that rat. That was not an option. *If I don't break free now, Raven's dead.*

Ever since he'd regained consciousness, he'd been flexing muscle groups up and down his body, grimly working to build a charge of power he could use to blast through the spell and tear free. Now he sent all that carefully hoarded power into his arms.

Instantly, his body seemed to turn to solid lead

as the spell fought his magic. *Yeah, bitch, I don't think so.* Never mind that Primo magic was supposed to be the weakest of all.

He shouldn't have been able to kill Gary either, so fuck that, and fuck *her.*

He dragged his head off the floor and fixed his gaze on Raven. As if feeling his stare, her eyes flicked to meet his…

And in those beautiful green eyes, he saw her love and fear and desperation -- and her utter willingness to die for him if that was what it took.

"Don't look at him, bitch!" Ewan snapped, pausing, one foot inches from Nate's bound arm. "You are *mine*! And I'm going to prove it to you again. But this time, you won't survive to run your fucking mouth!"

The image of that photo seemed to explode in Nate's mind: Raven, lying unconscious and bloodied in the floor, her shattered forearm bent into a sickening J.

Fury detonated through his brain, slamming into the leaden weight of Crystal's spell. He grabbed that anger, built it, let it rage, then blended it with the raw will and discipline his father had pounded into his head. And tried to summon his magic.

As it had before, the spell crushed down on him like a lead blanket. He set his teeth and kept pushing, fighting the vicious pressure.

Raven's gaze met his through the spell. He saw the love and despair in her beautiful green eyes…

And remembered the dying squeal of the rat.

Fuck. This. He threw all his will, all his love, all his rage at the spell, mixing it with his iron determination that *by God, she would not die*! And the working shattered, sigils bursting in a shower of sparks. Crystal screamed in shock and pain as her magic backlashed.

With a triumphant roar, Nate blasted his freed magic into every muscle in his arms and torso, and surged upward. Tape tore with an explosive riiiiip just as Ewan started to turn at the sound of Crystal's scream.

Nate grabbed the Bard's ankle in both hands and twisted in opposite directions with the same brutal strength that had shattered the Feral tiger's skull.

Bone snapped.

With a startled shriek, the Bard crashed to the ground. "Shit!"

"How's it feel, fucker?" Nate roared, and grabbed Ewan's belt, dragging the man into range with one hand as he gathered his magic in the other fist. He'd never actually tried to shatter someone's skull, but if he could punch his gun into a bulletproof tiger…

Out of the corner of one eye, he saw a flash of light off a knife blade, heard Crystal's shriek of sheer rage, the sound competing with Ewan's howls of pain.

He released the Bard and swung his arm up to knock the butcher knife aside before she could bury it in his chest. Screaming in fury, Crystal threw herself on him, landing astride his belly hard enough to knock the wind out of him. Her face set in a rictus of fury, she lifted the knife for another go at gutting him.

Nate grabbed her knife wrist and twisted, trying to wrench the blade from her hand, but Merlin gave her far more strength than she should have. Not to mention all the damn rats she'd sacrificed…

Raven began to sing. Her voice rose so high and pure that even as he fought to keep Crystal from burying her knife in his throat, magic-induced longing surged through him. It was an intoxicating craving, a need to be with Raven, as she poured all her magic into her song, trying to bewitch both his captors.

"No, you don't, bitch!" Ewan lunged to his feet as if he no longer felt the ankle Nate had broken.

Fucking Merlin.

"We're wearing charms, you stupid cunt! Just like you are, so I guess I can't use my magic either. I'll just have to beat you to death the way I should have years ago."

* * *

"Raven!" She heard her friends screaming her name from the wrong side of their spell prison. Unable to reach her. Unable to help.

Raven met Ewan's vicious stare as he staggered toward her. Her song choked off as her entire body froze in remembered pain. The beatings -- the blows to the ribs, the belly, the back of the head, so careful not to bruise her face or throat, nothing that would show on stage…

She'd never been able to make him stop. Not even with her magic.

"I told you you don't have anywhere near the Talent you think you do," he snarled, shoulders bunching, breath coming ragged as he limped over the ring of rats. "I can make you do any damn thing I want to. Because you're *weak*. You're as weak as my father always said I was. Well, I proved the bastard wrong, didn't I? I'm going to drag you into that circle, and I'm going to beat you to death the way I should have all those years ago. Then Crystal's going to take the magic of your life and *heal* me." He grabbed her wrist, bony fingers crushing brutally tight. Turning, he started hauling her back toward the circle.

Raven braced her feet, fighting his hold. He staggered, his ankle threatening to give under him.

She knew what she should do. *She knew.* Knew

she should fight back. Yet every time she'd ever tried to fight him, the beatings had only gotten worse. He'd conditioned her so thoroughly that her muscles wouldn't obey even as her mind screamed in futility and rage.

Nate bellowed, a shout of pain, though Raven couldn't see what had happened with Ewan in the way.

"Yeah!" Crystal screamed. "Eat that, fucker!"

"I'm gonna kill you, bitch!" Bruce roared. "I'm gonna hunt your ass down and I'm going to make you pay!"

"Raven!" Kara screamed, her voice raw with fear.

Crystal laughed, an ugly bark of triumph.

No, Raven thought, as rage stormed in and hit her fear. *No. Fuck, no! They are not killing Nate. And Ewan is Goddamn not killing me!* The terrified paralysis shattered like an eggshell. She whipped her hand back, found the pistol tucked into a pancake holster at her spine, and jerked it out.

Ewan didn't notice, too busy looking back at his accomplice. "Save something to sacrifice, Crystal! I'll get this one..." He turned back to her, drawing back his fist.

Raven shoved the .22 up under his chin. "Fuck you."

Eyes widening, he tried to jerk away.

She pulled the trigger.

The blast slapped her ears so hard they rang. Ewan toppled without a sound.

Raven didn't spare him another glance, just leaped over his body and ran for Crystal, who'd looked up from her struggle with Nate, knife in hand, at the sound of gunfire. Her shocked gaze found Ewan lying in a heap. "Ewan!" She sprang to her feet, knife lifted as she lunged at Raven. "You bitch!"

Raven had a heartbeat to wonder if she'd be able to hit a moving target.

Nate twisted and grabbed her legs, sending her tumbling. Shrieking, she swung the knife at his throat. He jerked aside and punched her in the mouth.

"Asshole!" Crystal shrieked as the knife flew from her hand.

"Quit it!" Raven swooped and rammed the muzzle of the pistol against the Arc's forehead. "You've already given me a reason," she snarled. "And I'm really fucking tempted."

Crystal froze, her eyes rolling to stare up at the gun pressed to her forehead. She raised her hands. "Okay, okay! Don't shoot!"

Raven glanced at Nate. "You oka..." She broke off. The entire front of his chest was wet with blood. "*Nate!*"

"I'm fine," he panted, which was an obvious fucking lie. "We need to... get her to let Bruce and the girls... past her damned spell circle."

Her gaze swung back to Crystal, and she damned near pulled the trigger. "You'd better not even breathe until the cops arrive or I'm going to blow your damn head off. Given the shit you pulled, all we have to do is show them your little circle of dead rats. They'd file your death under saving the state of California an execution. *Drop that spell circle!*"

Her terrified gaze focused on Raven's furious eyes, the Arcanist obeyed.

* * *

While Monique called 911 from the phone in the kitchen, Bruce had used his Marine-trained first aid skill to bandage Nate's chest wound with clean bar towels he'd cut into strips.

Meanwhile, Raven and Kara duct-taped the Arcanist to a chair.

Nate had begun to wheeze, and there was a bubbling sound to his breathing that had her scared out of her mind. He was unconscious by the time EMTs loaded him onto the gurney.

The cops refused to let Raven go with him. She came within an inch of using her voice to compel them, but she was in enough trouble without adding felony magical influence on law enforcement. So she kept her mouth shut and forced herself to watch with burning eyes as they wheeled him out.

* * *

Thirty hours later, Raven sat in an exhausted slump next to Nate's hospital bed. Her head throbbed, and her stomach growled. She ignored both. She'd been so terrified for him, she hadn't slept or eaten.

She'd missed the surgery to save his life. Since her fingerprints were on the gun that shot Ewan and there'd been no convenient video to prove his death was self-defense, she'd been in a holding cell at the L.A. County jail at the time.

That is, when she wasn't answering questions from detectives, her own lawyer, and a magistrate until she felt wrung out and numb. At least it had paid off. She, Bruce, Monique and Kara were all out on bail now.

Crystal was still locked up, thank God. Not only were her prints on the knife she'd used to stab Nate, but the LAPD's Arcanist had confirmed the magic lingering around the sacrificial spell circle was definitely hers. The judge hadn't been inclined to let anyone suspected of felony magical sacrifice run loose.

Bruce and Monique had staggered back to their respective homes to get some sleep. Raven's law firm and Bard Records' PR team were working on the statement she would read to the media.

Since, again, there was no video, the scandal had hit her professional life like a Cat Five hurricane. They were all going to have to work through the process. Luckily Nate hadn't been charged -- his role as human sacrifice was obvious from the duct tape adhesive still clinging to his skin when he'd been taken to the hospital.

The cops had found plenty of physical evidence. There were the magic circles and the knife, with its mix of rat and human blood, though getting the DNA samples analyzed would take weeks. Still, necroscopies had proved most of the rats had been killed at the bar while Nate, Raven, and Kara were still on live TV.

Crystal had claimed she and Ewan were being framed, but she'd told so many contradicting stories, she'd only looked more guilty.

One of the detectives had said privately that he doubted Raven would be charged in Ewan's death, especially given the cops knew her ex had lied like hell during his interview on *LA Morning*.

Nothing he'd said reflected what the cops knew had actually happened, so he'd obviously been playing games. Especially since the autopsy had revealed he did indeed have cancer, and the spell circle they'd been planning to sacrifice Ewan and Raven in had a healing component.

Crystal was in deep shit.

Raven rubbed her eyes wearily, then flicked a look at Nate's sleeping face. With a sigh, she reached over to wrap her fingers around his wrist, craving the reassuring warmth of his skin, the feeling of his pulse beating against her fingers.

Nate's all right, she told herself. *He survived and so*

did the rest of us. We can handle the rest of the bullshit.

"What are *you* doing here, witch?" a female voice demanded.

Startled, Raven looked up as a middle-aged woman stormed into the room, tall and blonde, deep shadows under her eyes. "I should've known I'd find you here!"

Raven blinked at her numbly. Her brain felt as if her thoughts were trapped in molasses from sheer exhaustion. "Do I know you?"

"As if I'd have anything to do with *you*." The woman glared at her as a tall middle-aged man walked in behind her. Must be her husband.

Raven's gaze flicked to his face and the penny finally dropped. She knew that square jaw, the angle of the nose, the cool eyes. "Oh, you're his parents."

"Yes, we're his parents. And unlike *you*, we have a right to be here." The woman thrust a finger at Nate, who still lay sleeping off his latest surgery. "And *you're* the reason he's in that hospital bed. You and your whoring around with some psycho. Trafficking in magic. Get the hell out. You're not wanted here!"

Raven stared at her blearily, too damn tired for this. She was also too damn tired to run the gauntlet of media surrounding the hospital, but it seemed she was going to have to face them anyway. Wearily, she released Nate's hand and started to climb to her feet.

Before she could move away, long, warm fingers wrapped around hers and held on. "No, she's not leaving." Nate's voice sounded gravelly with sleep. "And you're right, she *is* the reason I'm here."

Wait, he blamed her? But…

"Because if not for her, I'd be in the morgue."

His mother stared at him for a startled moment before her face lit with relief as if she'd forgotten all about Raven. "Oh my God, Nate, we were terrified! How are you feeling? Is there anything we can get you? We would've been here earlier, except there was a storm and we couldn't get a flight, and then we spent hours at the airport and…"

"Raven," Nate interrupted. She looked down to see him frowning up at her. "Sit down before you drop on the floor. You look like it's all you can do to remain conscious. You've got another migraine, haven't you?"

Raven's gaze flicked from his mother's face to her to his. She cleared her throat. "Maybe I ought to just let y'all catch up. I can go down and get something to eat. Haven't eaten since… Since you were hurt." She broke off and frowned. "What time is it?"

Nate's father considered her thoughtfully. "Eight o'clock. I assume you're the reason he's got this private room."

"Well, yeah. Otherwise, the paparazzi would be in here."

"Yes, we know," his mother snapped, whipping from loving mother to raging mama bear in 4.23 seconds. "We had to fight our way through a pack of them just to get in the hospital. So yes, leave. And don't come back."

Now Nate's expression went cold. "I repeat, *Raven saved my life.* I was duct-taped to the floor, under a spell, and about to be a human sacrifice. She showed up at that bar knowing Ewan intended to kill her so she could rescue me. And when he trapped Bruce and her friends on the other side of a magic circle, she fought him, even though he'd beaten her for years. To. Save. *Me.*"

Uncomfortable, Raven pointed out, "You freed yourself, Nate." To his parents she added, "He used his power to rip out of the magic Crystal bound him with, then snapped the duct tape and fought her. And got stabbed doing it. If there's a hero in this mess, he's it. Just like he saved us all from that Feral..." She frowned, trying to remember if it had been yesterday or the day before. She'd completely lost track of time.

"Which would've done me zero good if you hadn't shown up. They'd have killed me before I had a chance to get away." He returned his attention to his parents. "So Raven has a right to stay here. And you'd better get used to it, because I'm in love with her, and I'm going to marry her." He blinked and his gaze flew to hers, as if he'd said more than he'd intended. Clearing his throat, he added, "Assuming she'll have me."

Raven froze and looked at him, her jaw dropping. "What?"

He winced. "I completely hosed that up, didn't I? I was supposed to propose first." To his parents, he said, "Just... pretend you didn't hear that."

"Yes." Raven dropped to her knees beside the bed and took his hand in hers as tears flooded her eyes. "Yes, I'll marry you." She broke off to study his face. "If you meant it."

"He didn't." His mother glowered. "This has got to be the drugs talking. How much morphine do they have you on? You've got to be high if you'd propose to this little..."

Nate's father, who'd been looking at Nate's face, grabbed her hand. "Darling, I think it's time you shut up now. We're the ones who should go down to the cafeteria and get something to eat."

"But..."

He tugged her firmly toward the door. "We'll get the story later. Cafeteria now."

She looked over her shoulder at them. "Nate, you

can't really mean to…"

Nate sighed. "Love you, Mom. We'll talk later."

His father closed the door firmly behind them, but their raised voices were still audible out in the hallway. "She's put some kind of spell on him!"

"Yeah, the same one you laid on me thirty-six years ago. He's in love with her. Guys don't take on bulletproof tigers for women they're not in love with. You saw that video."

"But…" Their voices faded.

"I hope nobody hears that," Raven told Nate. "Or they're going to be the front page of *The Enquirer* tomorrow."

"Maybe it'll teach them to be a little more damned discreet." His gaze searched hers. "Did you mean it, that yes? It's not gratitude talking?"

"Nobody's grateful enough to step into a sacrificial circle for someone they don't love." She looked at him and enunciated clearly so there would be no doubt. "I meant every damned word. I love you. I want to marry you."

He reared up to reach for her, then grunted in pain and fell back, grabbing at his chest.

"Nate!" She looked frantically for the nurse call button. She was about to lunge for it when he caught her shoulders.

"I'm fine," he told her. "It was just a twinge."

Raven glowered. "That didn't look like a twinge. That looked like…"

He pulled her down into a kiss. It was hot and wet with as much tenderness as desire, and Raven felt the slow bloom of belief, of joy spreading through her body like a flight of butterflies.

"Oh God, Nate, I thought…" Her voice broke as she cupped his stubbled face in both hands. "When he took you…" A tear spilled down her face. "I thought I'd lost you. I thought you were dead."

He brushed the tear away with his thumb. "I thought I'd lost you too. I couldn't break free from that damn spell, and I was afraid he'd kill you before…"

"Do you really think I was so dumb I wouldn't bring a gun?"

He snorted. "Luckily, Ewan didn't think you'd have a gun either."

"He hadn't had me on the range every day for the past year and a half," Raven pointed out. Then her smile faded. "But… I think your mom has a point - that 'yes' needs to be provisional. Ask me again in a week when you're not taking pain meds."

He snorted. "I knew I was going to propose when I was lying in that circle, listening to you follow every one of that crazy bastard's instructions to all those payphones. Nobody would've done that except someone who loved me. I'm just surprised you didn't realize he intended to sacrifice both of us."

"Oh, I knew exactly what he was going to do," Raven said. "I just didn't give a damn, because if I couldn't get you out, I didn't care what happened to me."

"Goddamn it, Raven!"

She lifted a blonde brow. "Which one of us jumped the psycho Arc despite the chest wound pumping blood like a fountain?"

"Well, yeah -- I love you." He didn't sound in the least stoned. "I love you." And he kissed her again, all tongue and heat.

The glowing, effervescent joy took her by surprise. It was far more intense than anything she'd ever felt in her life, including the night she'd won so many Grammys, it was all she could do not to drop them.

With a soft moan, Raven kissed him back, her tongue swirling around his as he wrapped his arms around her. She braced her hands on the mattress, trying to avoid putting pressure on their wounds, and gave the kiss everything she had.

When they finally drew apart again, she combed her fingers through his tangled curls. "I hate to tell you this, but we're going to have one hell of a wedding."

He blinked at that. "We are? Because I was thinking we'd elope."

"I'm *not* sneaking off to Vegas." Her eyes narrowed. "This time all the lace and silk and candles are going to be real. This time we're getting a happily ever after."

Epilogue

The engagement lasted more than a year. Aside from the planning, scheduling, and preparation, there'd been the legal mess to straighten out. Crystal had been tried and convicted in late January, a bit less than a year after the crime. Normally, of course, a murder case could drag on for years, but the federal government didn't fuck around when it came to human sacrifice.

There'd been a ton of physical evidence -- Crystal's prints on the knife, Nate's and the rats' blood on the blade, and the testimony of the LAPD Arcanist that the spell circle had been Crystal's. The bar's owner had testified that Crystal and Ewan had rented Will Scarlet's the day before, while a Hertz clerk confirmed they'd also rented the van they'd used in the kidnapping. As Nate had dryly observed, "Planning a ritual human sacrifice high on Merlin is a really bad idea." He, along with Raven, Bruce, Kara and Monique had all testified in the televised trial, winning a lot of public sympathy in the process.

When Raven's album -- renamed *Magic Hands* -- had finally been released in February, it had promptly gone platinum. The *Magic Hands* single -- which hit number one on *Billboard* -- was, of course, about Nate. The album did *not* include "Your Feral Heart," the song the video had been intended to promote. Raven doubted she'd ever sing it again. She still had nightmares about that day, though waking up in Nate's arms helped.

* * *

The notes of the "Prince of Denmark's March" rose on the spring air as Raven's heavy white silk skirts rustled softly over the grass like a lace bow wave. The off-the-shoulder bodice glittered with seed pearls, and on either side, the wedding guests seated in the Italian villa's garden murmured with appreciation.

She had one hand tucked in Jonathan Mayfield's elbow as he escorted her down the aisle. Kara's dad looked tall and distinguished in his black tailcoat and trousers, his white bow tie, shirt and vest dazzling against his dark skin.

Raven stared through her veil toward the Gothic arch decked with masses of roses and white gardenias where Nate waited with the priest, looking handsome and healthy again in his tux.

Bruce stood by his side as best man, while Roger served as one of his groomsmen, a prosthetic arm filling the left sleeve of his tailcoat. The director still looked a bit thin and pale, but he was doing much better, especially since Raven intended to use him on her future videos. It wasn't pity. Roger was a damned good director, asshole or not.

Nate's other military buddies rounded out the groomsmen, while Kara was Raven's maid of honor in a breathtaking designer gown in buttercup yellow that looked incredible against her rich, dark skin. Monique looked just as beautiful among the other bridesmaids.

Raven was barely aware of anything beyond the love in Nate's gray eyes as they recited their vows. Somehow they managed their wedding rings without either band getting stuck on a knuckle, and the Catholic priest declared them man and wife.

The reception was a blur of very good wine and an impressive selection of food, all set up under the villa's four-hundred-year-old portico with its gothic arches and garden view. Raven and Nate spent the afternoon feeding each other bites of cake and assorted exotic delicacies.

She tossed the bouquet -- Monique caught it -- then danced with Nate as darkness fell, happier than she'd been in her life.

* * *

"Enough of this dog and pony show," Nate murmured in her ear when they'd finished yet another waltz. "I want quality time with my wife."

With that, he scooped her into his arms, miles of skirt and all, and swept her through the doors into the villa. Kara, laughing, chased after them to snatch up Raven's train before he tripped on it. She piled the expensive silk into Raven's arms, and they were off.

Nate carried her into the villa and up the sweeping staircase to the raucous cheers of family and friends. Raven laughed in sheer joy as he climbed, giddy as a kid on Christmas morning who'd gotten the promised pony. "Put me down before you kill your back!"

"You underestimate me." He gave her a slow, hot grin. "I could carry you all day."

And then he proceeded to prove it, striding through the villa's upstairs corridors as though she weighed no more than a two-year-old. When they reached the door to their very elegant bedroom, he dipped her so she could turn the knob, then toed the door open and bore her inside.

The first thing they saw was an enormous window displaying a dazzling view of the sea, light dancing over the dark water beneath a blazing sunset in shades of gold, orange, and red, shading up into violet.

Nate lifted her higher and bent his head for a kiss, slow and demanding, his tongue swirling around hers with possessive hunger. His mouth tasted of champagne and strawberries and desire. Raven hooked her arms around his neck, moaning in delight as their mutual need spun them into a whirlwind of craving.

Her nipples peaked against the silk of her bodice as her pussy grew slick.

Finally, Nate lifted his head and smiled down at her, rocking back and forth, so that the skirt of her gown swayed with the movement as it spilled over his arms.

"That dress is very pretty…" he told her, "… but it needs to go." Releasing her legs, he let her slide down his body. Feeling the thick bulk of his cock against her belly, she caught her breath in anticipation.

When her high heels finally touched the floor, Raven leaned into him, her gaze dwelling on his handsome face, tight and sculpted with need, his gray eyes burning into hers. Her heart was pounding hard now, and her stiff nipples raked across the silk of her bodice every time she inhaled, her craving intensifying as her breathing grew rough. "You're going to have to help me with the zipper," she said, her voice a little rough with the relentless build of heat. Gathering up her voluminous skirts, she turned.

"This dress is a torture device."

Raven grimaced, feeling the bite of the boned bodice. "Yeah, I've worn some uncomfortable costumes, but this thing…"

"No, I mean alllll this fabric. In between me and your pretty, pretty body." He leaned down and kissed the nape of her neck, then scraped his teeth over the slope of her shoulder. Closed them in a gentle bite. As she shivered, she listened to the seductive hiss as he unzipped the dress. Raven shivered, letting her head fall back.

Nate started tugging the gown down, kissing the widening V of skin he revealed. The warmth of his lips made her quiver, eyes sliding shut as her arousal began a slow sizzle like a fuse burning beneath her skin.

Finally he drew the dress all the way down the curve of her hips and the length of her legs until she was able to step out of the puddle of silk, lace, and seed pearls. She turned and had the satisfaction of seeing his eyes widen.

The white silk demi bra she wore mounded her breasts high, nipples barely veiled by lace as delicate as a spiderweb. Panties even thinner veiled her pubes, framed by a white garter belt that supported white stockings with lace appliqués decorating the top and calves.

Her eyes dipped, and she saw he really, *really* approved of the view. His cock tented his tux trousers, looking more than a little like a tree limb. Smiling in anticipation, Raven stepped against him and curled one arm around his neck, caressing the curve of his ear, leaning in until she pressed against his hard shaft. Grinning, she rolled against him, deliberately slow and wicked. "Yuuuuuum."

He laughed. "And this is why I kept wishing the front of the damn tailcoat was longer. I was afraid everyone would see I'd sprung wood."

"More like redwood," she teased, twitching her hips back and forth against his erection as she reached up to untie his bow tie. By the time she pulled it from around his neck and tossed it on the bedside table, he'd already shrugged out of his jacket.

Nate's gaze rested hungrily on her face, her lips, then drifted down to the cleavage the bra displayed. He stepped back a pace to get the full effect, letting his eyes drift lower to the tiny panties, down her stocking-clad legs to her crystal-encrusted white stilettos. She cocked a hip, knowing the shoes made her legs look a mile long.

"Gotta say, that outfit makes this whole insane day worth it."

Raven lifted her eyebrows at him. "Marrying me was insane?"

He grinned. "Oh, hell no. What was insane was the three-ring circus I had to endure to do it. Though I did enjoy Kara's magical phoenix whirling around us on the dance floor. Most people just release doves."

"Most people don't have Kara's imagination." She started unbuttoning his vest, then slid it off his wide shoulders to reveal the fine linen shirt he wore under it. He was already working on one onyx cufflink engraved with his initials, his fingers deliciously big and competent as he slid the studs free and tossed them on the bureau with a musical rattle.

"Mmmm." Raven began unbuttoning the shirt, spreading the fabric to reveal his hard, muscled torso, pausing to run her manicured nails through his ruff of chest hair.

But as she brushed the shirt off his shoulders, her gaze fell on the scars left by Crystal's knife -- and the surgery that had saved him. Leaning in, she kissed each one. "I'm so sorry," she murmured.

"Worth it."

Raven looked up at him and grinned. "Why do I get the feeling that you found the wedding circus more traumatic than the stabbing?"

"Probably because you know me." He shook his head. "We've been together almost three years now, but I'm still not used to rubbing shoulders with Madonna and Elton fucking John."

"Let me tell you a secret…" She traced her fingers over the curve of one pectoral down to a flat nipple, which peaked under the tender rake of her nails. He made a delighted rumble of approval and reached down to run his own fingers over the rise of her breast. "I've been doing the rock star bit for years now, and I'm not used to it either. It's insane."

He chuckled and started unbuckling his belt. "Funny, you didn't look intimidated."

"I'm a better actress than the critics give me credit for." She reached for the zipper of his slacks, dropping gracefully to her knees like the dancer she was. He dropped the belt and watched, a smile curving his lips as she started tugging down the slacks…

And burst out laughing. "You're kidding!"

He was wearing a pair of white silk boxers with her band's logo: a woman's bright red mouth, teeth sunk into her lower lip, framed by raven wings. The words "Property of Raven," ran underneath it from hip to hip, right across the bulge of his erection. The band sold the novelty boxers as concert merchandise, along with T-shirts and CDs. "You actually bought this? And wore it *today*?"

He grinned and sat down on the bed to take off his socks and dress shoes. "Well, I figured you'd get a kick out of it."

"Oh, I fucking *love* it." She narrowed her eyes up at him. "And it's true, too." Cupping one hand possessively over his logo-covered cock, she growled, "Mine, mine, mine, mine!"

"It is that." Nate laughed and finished pulling his pants off, but when he reached for the boxers, she grabbed the waistband herself. "Oh, no. I'm doing the honors." He lifted himself on his hands to let her pull them off, grinning wickedly.

She pulled them down slowly, leaning in to kiss the bared head of his shaft, then pulling the silken boxers lower to catch under his balls. The fabric lifted them higher, and she eyed them hungrily. One by one, she took each warm, furry testicle into her mouth for a long, slow suck. With a shuddering groan, he fell back on the mattress to brace on his elbows, eyes blazing as he watched her down the length of his impressive body.

Raven's lips curled and she began to hum, pouring waves of deep vibration into his balls. Using her magic to caress him.

Nate made a strangled sound, his head falling back as his hands hit the comforter and fisted as if he fought for control.

Oh, baby, I'm just getting started. She sucked and hummed until his hips started to pump. Releasing his balls with a juicy pop, she began licking her way up his cock, humming again, using her magic to stoke his lust even more. When she reached the head of his erection, she started to slide her mouth down over it…

Only to yelp in surprise as he surged off the bed and scooped her into his arms, then sat down again with her in his lap, ass landing on his hard-on.

"You," he growled, "are wearing way too many clothes. Pretty as they are." He slid his arms around her and unhooked her bra with a few skilled flicks of his fingers.

She grinned. "Why do I get the feeling you've done that a time or two?"

He snorted. "I'd hope so." He tossed the bra aside, then eyed the full curves of her breasts as she watched in hot anticipation.

He winced a little as he saw the red marks the tight bra had left in her soft skin. "Damn, woman, that looks painful."

"I've worn worse," she told him dryly.

He snorted. "Like that spiked thing for the VMAs. I was worried you were going to put your own eye out." Then he lowered his head and started kissing the indentations, licking and nibbling until she was lost in the heat of his skilled mouth, the swirl of his tongue that made her roll her hips in building lust.

But he avoided her nipples. Damn it.

It wasn't long before he had her writhing just as hard as she'd had him.

Next came the tiny panties, though she could tell he was seriously tempted to rip those in two. He tugged them down her legs, leaving her only in the stockings and heels. He straightened, rocking back on his knees as he stared hungrily down at her. "God, you're beautiful," he said hoarsely, only to wave the sentence away with a crooked smile. "Like you don't hear that all the time."

Raven met his gaze and told him, "It doesn't matter coming from anyone but you."

That made his smile turn even hotter. She opened her arms to him, and he fell into them, swooping in for a kiss. It was wet and needy and so deliciously erotic that her nipples stirred his chest hair, a deliciously ticklish sensation. Their tongues danced lazily as love rose in her, more intense and overwhelming even that the furious urgency of her desire.

Nate began to kiss his way down her chin, her throat, his hands stroking over her body, teasing her arousal even higher.

"My turn now," she gasped, her hands gripping his short sable curls.

He ignored her completely, his mouth going

even more greedily on her aching flesh. For a moment, she was tempted to use her voice on him, but she instantly killed the impulse.

She was never going to do that to him again. Not ever. He wasn't Ewan and she didn't need to control him. He would never do anything to hurt her.

That skillful tongue finally discovered one aching nipple and began to lick her like ice cream before he closed his teeth around it for a sizzling series of little rakes. Then he engulfed it in his mouth in slow, exquisite pulls that zinged straight to her pussy. She rolled her head back, gasping, one hand finding his head, combing through the sable silk of his hair. She caught one muscled shoulder with the other, digging in her nails. He cupped her other breast and suckled even harder, sending pulse after pulse of pleasure rolling up her body. "God," she gasped. "God, that feels good."

Releasing her grip on his hair, she slid her hands to every part of him she could reach, fingertips tracing the thick, working muscle of his biceps, the sweeping line of his shoulders. A spray of tiny divots that must be shrapnel scars.

He could have died, and I'd have never known him. Never touched him. Never loved him. Never known his love. The chilling thought made her nails dig into his smooth, tanned skin.

Before she could get sucked even deeper into that line of thought, he was working his way down her body, one hand sliding between her thighs, slipping into the cleft of her labia. "God, you're so wet." The deep, hungry rumble made her shiver.

"I've been wet most of the day." Her lips twitched. "You looked really good in that tux. But you look even better naked." She danced her nails down his broad back, flattened her hands to cup the curve of his bare ass. "Oooh, yeah. Gettin' even wetter."

He flashed a grin up her body. "I always liked that song. It was one long double entendre."

She smirked. "It's not just a song."

"Yeah?" He shot her blonde pussy a hungry look. "I think that calls for a taste test." Rolling between her thighs, he slid down her torso, making her groan at the feeling of all that hard masculinity pressing against her much smaller, much softer body.

"Hey, I wanna eat too." Though it came out sounding more strangled than seductive. "And that pants python of yours has been driving me nuts all day."

He paused to lift a brow. "'Pants python? Aren't you supposed to be the Bard of LA?"

"God, that reporter was pretentious as hell." She let her grin go lascivious. "On the other hand, us LA girls have all kinds of skills…"

He laughed. "Oh, I know. Which is why you ain't doing any snake eating. Yet, anyway. I want to this to take a long, *long* time."

"Awww, come on! It's only fair. And you're not the only one who wants a taste."

He was able to withstand her best big-eyed pleading look for less than thirty seconds. "No more humming! I'm damned if I'm going to embarrass myself on our wedding night."

She grinned, thinking of all the times they'd made love over the past year. "Darling, that's never been a problem. I think maybe we should do this on our sides. Last time I got a crick in my neck." They rearranged themselves, Raven propping on an elbow to use the other hand to angle his impressive cock toward her mouth.

Only to freeze, her eyes almost crossing as his fingers slipped between her labia and spread them wide. His curls brushed her belly as his tongue slicked across her clit, then lapped to either side, seeking out sensitive bundles of nerves, flicking and teasing. And every wet, delicate stroke sent darts of searing pleasure up her spine until the muscles in her thighs began to twitch.

Mind-blowing as that was, she was determined to give him as much pleasure as he gave her. She leaned in, wrapping a hand around his thick cock and angling the shaft so she could take him deep. One thing a singer knew was breath control, and she used that knowledge ruthlessly as she engulfed inch after inch of broad shaft.

When she heard him gasp, the corners of her stuffed mouth twitched in an attempted smile. Then she began to pull, sucking hard even as he licked and nibbled and did his considerable best to drive her insane.

* * *

With that delicious mouth wrapped around his cock, sucking until his eyes lost focus, it was all Nate could do to concentrate on giving Raven the pleasure she deserved. Fortunately, he loved the taste and scent and feel of her concentrated passion.

He took the lush, erotic torment as long as he could, fighting his own clawing hunger, but his self-control was steadily unraveling. He didn't want to risk losing it too soon. He pulled away from her, though she laughed and grabbed his cock. "Mine!"

"It certainly is," he growled, and pounced, rolling her onto her back. She grinned up at him as he settled onto one braced elbow and started feeding it into her slick heat.

Her green eyes widened, and they both groaned as he slid slowly home. She felt so wet, all slick silk and grip and heat. He fought the instinct to close his eyes, wanting to watch her beautiful face as he made love to his wife for the first time.

He knew he'd remember this moment until his dying day.

Her eyes looked enormous, pupils blown huge and dazed by pleasure. He kissed her, swallowing her moans as he thrust, slowly, taking his time. Her cunt clamped his cock, so sweet. So hot. So perfect.

She rolled up to meet him, her long legs clad in those stockings wrapping around his ass. He'd always loved her legs, particularly in those sky-high heels she always wore. How the woman danced in them was anybody's guess.

His beautiful fairy queen.

Nate controlled his need to plunge with ruthless discipline as her eyes lost focus and drifted closed. Her parted lips were bare of lipstick -- his cock was wearing most of it -- open in a gasping O. Nate began to lengthen his plunging, ruthless strokes, feeling her inner muscles clenching in pulsing contractions as she built toward orgasm. He could feel his balls drawing tight to his shaft, urgent heat building, on the verge of a blazing explosion.

"Nate!" Raven arched hard in his arms, writhing against him.

He growled and rolled on his back, dragging her with him, and started grinding hard, and fast, holding nothing back until the fire came blazing up from his balls to drown him in a blazing climax.

Raven cried out, magic ringing in her voice, giving his name a power he'd never heard before. "*Nate!*" A one-word song of love and delight.

Nate bellowed back, "God, I love you. Love you, love you, love you!"

And the fire took them both.

* * *

He collapsed back on the mattress with Raven draped over him, both thoroughly drained. They lay there in exquisite peace, panting and sweetly wrung out.

As he concentrated on breathing, Nate stroked his hands through her hair, and she lifted her head to look down at him. "I guess I finally did it." She leaned in so close her lips moved against his as she whispered, "*I found love.*"

"*We* found love," he told her. "And we're never going to lose it."

Author's Note -- Timeline

In our universe, the 1991 military conflict called Desert Storm lasted only 43 days. But in the Arcane Talents universe, the fight to drive Saddam Hussein's invading Iraqi forces out of Kuwait lasted for a year and a half. Most of the additional time was because Iraq's magic-using Republican Guard was able to compensate for the air superiority of the U.S. and its allies. The allies eventually won, but the fight dragged on much longer than it would have if not for magic, and American casualties were significant.

Angela Knight

New York Times best-selling author Angela Knight has written and published more than sixty novels, novellas, and ebooks, including the Mageverse and Merlin's Legacy series. With a career spanning more than two decades, Romantic Times Bookclub Magazine has awarded her their Career Achievement award in Paranormal Romance, as well as two Reviewers' Choice awards for Best Erotic Romance and Best Werewolf Romance.

Angela is currently a writer, editor, and cover artist for Changeling Press LLC. She also teaches online writing courses. Besides her fiction work, Angela's writing career includes a decade as an award-winning South Carolina newspaper reporter. She lives in South Carolina with her husband, Michael, a thirty-year police veteran and detective with a local police department.

Angela at Changeling: changelingpress.com/angela-knight-a-26

Changeling Press E-Books

More Sci-Fi, Fantasy, Paranormal, and BDSM adventures available in e-book format for immediate download at ChangelingPress.com -- Werewolves, Vampires, Dragons, Shapeshifters and more -- Erotic Tales from the edge of your imagination.

What are E-Books?

E-books, or electronic books, are books designed to be read in digital format -- on your desktop or laptop computer, notebook, tablet, Smart Phone, or any electronic e-book reader.

Where can I get Changeling Press E-Books?

Changeling Press e-books are available at ChangelingPress.com, Amazon, Apple Books, Barnes & Noble, and Kobo/Walmart.

Changeling Press, LLC

ChangelingPress.com